2

PARKED UP

Janet Hunter

4

SUGGESTED SOUNDTRACK

1. Green Onions – *Booker T and the MGs*
2. Go Steady – *The Lambrettas*
3. Going to a Go-Go – *The Miracles*
4. I heard it through the Grapevine – *Marvin Gaye*
5. Footsee – *Wigan's Chosen Few*
6. Wade in the Water – *Ramsey Lewis*
7. Out on the Floor – *Dobie Gray*
8. Shake a Tail Feather – *James and Bobby Purify*
9. You're Gonna Make Me Love You – *Sandi Sheldon*
10. Let's Go Baby (Where the Action Is) – *Robert Parker*
11. Red Light Spells Danger – *Billy Ocean*
12. Come See About Me – *The Supremes*
13. Sliced Tomatoes – *Just Brothers*
14. Rescue Me – *Fontella Bass*
15. Breakin' Down the Walls of Heartache – *Johnny Johnson and the Bandwagon*
16. Just a Little Misunderstanding – *The Contours*
17. (I'm a) Roadrunner – *Junior Walker and the All Stars*

18. The Night – *Frankie Valli and the Four Seasons*
19. Long After Tonight is All Over – *Irma Thomas*
20. Love on a Mountain Top – *Robert Knight*
21. There's a Ghost in my House – *R Dean Taylor*
22. Heatwave – *Martha Reeves and the Vandellas*
23. Right Track – *Billy Butler*
24. Breakout – *Mitch Ryder and the Detroit Wheels*
25. Do I Love You (Indeed I Do) – *Frank Wilson*

7

8

Chapter One

There weren't many passengers on the bus. On a Wednesday evening in January most people were coming home from town rather than going into it, at least by public transport. I sat down at the front of the back. You could smoke there.

I fingered the packet of 10 Silk Cut in my pocket but decided against lighting up. I never knew what to do with the butt once I'd finished. Throwing it out the window or sticking it in my pocket seemed to be the only two options, neither of which appealed. There weren't any bins even though the bus came equipped with something to stub your cigarette out on. This was a crosshatched metal object attached to the back of the seat in front. I remembered as a child being fascinated by the texture and coldness of it and Mum telling me off for trying to lick it.

Anyway I was still smarting from the comments made by a couple of fellow students on my college course. They said I didn't smoke properly, that I didn't take it into my lungs. I imagined everyone laughing at my failed attempts to look cool and had cut down quite drastically. I had tried the alternative – actually inhaling – and found I didn't like it much.

At the last stop in the village a girl of about my age got on. I didn't recognise her, which was strange, our school catchment meant that I knew pretty much everyone of my age within a five mile radius. Maybe she was new; she didn't look like a private school pupil and she certainly didn't act like one. She was dressed for summer rather than winter and had her hair scraped back in a tight, high ponytail. She parked herself right behind the driver, next to the 'Please do not talk to the driver whilst the bus is in motion' sign and began to flirt with him, smoothing her hair and fiddling with a hoop earring. I could see from his rear-view mirror that he was spending more time looking at her than concentrating on the road ahead.

I couldn't see the attraction myself, he was always cheerful and chatty but he was like that with everyone so you wouldn't mistake it for a personal interest. He had to be getting on for twice her age too so was probably married with kids. Maybe that was the thrill for her, I thought. It was interesting to watch though; I liked travelling by bus for that reason.

I wondered what other passengers would make of me. It was dark outside now so I could examine the reflection of myself in the window, actually two selves superimposed on one another due to the double layering of the glass. In it I looked quite miserable, a natural feature of my face it seemed, as strangers were often suggesting I cheer up (love). I experimented with lifting the corners of my mouth but it just succeeded in making me look slightly barmy. My best feature, I thought, was my hair. I had it cut in a sharp bob and had coloured it as red as you could get from a packet off the shelf at Boots which meant that it was orange really. Still it was an improvement on my natural mouse. My eyes were heavily rimmed with black eyeliner that I flicked out at the corners. Despite these attempts to create a sophisticated look, my face was wide and unthreatening and I still looked like a child rather than an adult.

My hair style suggested I was a Mod, or a Modette since that was the term for girl Mods, and I wore the clothes to match – pointy flat black shoes, black tights, short black skirt and a knitted twin-set. Most of this was hidden by my coat though – a US Army parka that I had bought the previous week in the local gents' outfitters. It was heavy and voluminous, being made for someone much taller and wider. It was the only one in the shop that didn't look completely ridiculous on. At first I rejected it as somewhere near the neck I discovered a finger-sized hole that had been carefully hemmed to stop it fraying.

'Is this a bullet hole?' I asked my friend June who had come along to assist with the purchase.

'Could be.'

'Do you think someone *died* in it?'

It being quiet in the shop, the assistant overheard our conversation and hurried over.

'It could be from all sorts of things, madam' he said. 'Maybe it was a cigarette burn, maybe he dozed off with his hood up and the cigarette slipped.'

'Anyway,' said June, poking her finger through the hole and examining the edges, 'there aren't any blood stains, and blood *stains.* I should know. So if it was caused by a bullet it can't have made it through to the person inside the coat, so maybe the coat saved his life.'

I liked the sound of a life-saving coat. I could do with something I could put on and be safe. The sale was assured.

I put my hands in the pockets and pulled the coat around me. Most Mods decorated their parkas. Some painted or drew 'The Jam' or 'The Who' logos on the back. Others had targets or Union Jacks and some sewed on beer towels nicked from pub counters.

So far the only adornment I had added to mine was a small Union Jack patch on one arm. I still wasn't sure that the parka made me a 'proper' Mod. It took more than clothes to be part of a group. I remembered how it was the quietest, straightest-laced boy at school who suddenly appeared mincing down the street in tartan bondage trousers (he'd done them up too tight) and tinkling with hundreds of safety pins. No one believed he actually *was* a punk, just someone dressed up as one.

Round our way, the Mod revival had been in full-swing since 1978, around the time that the film 'Quadrophenia' was released. I hadn't been able to see it as, at thirteen, I'd been too young and fresh-faced to fool the cinema attendant so I had had to content myself with stills from the film out of a copy of 'Smash Hits'. I had stuck the pictures on my wall and imagined that I was part of the group of characters all sauntering together down the front at Brighton. I was modelling myself on a boy with a scooter though rather than a girl who got a lift on one.

Three years later, we'd gone as a family to the South Coast for Easter and on the Monday had come across a large gathering of Mods on the seafront at Brighton. Scooters were parked up in rows while others were parading up and down the promenade. It was a sea of shiny paint and chrome and khaki clothing. Most of the Mods were male and many barely older than me. I tried hanging around them casually and pretending I wasn't with my family, but I knew if they saw me at all it was as a kid rather than an equal. My clothes, which I'd picked with such care, suddenly looked childish and wrong.

Back in our village most boys listened to Heavy Metal music and called themselves headbangers. They grew their hair long and wore band t-shirts. It wasn't a look that attracted girls in great numbers.

The few boys who became Mods stood out due to their neatness and cleanliness. Anyone with short hair and a sharp jacket and I was immediately interested. In my last year at school a new boy joined. He was already sixteen and rode in on a Vespa. He even did something with his school uniform to make it look smart in a way no one else managed. I was in awe of him and worked out the times I was likely to bump into him in the corridors. He never noticed me of course.

Once I left school and didn't have to wear a school uniform any longer I started to wear the Modette look as a new kind of uniform and finally I took the great leap of buying the parka. It made it clear who I was, or at least who I wanted to be and who I wanted to hang out with. The only problem was a proper Mod rode a scooter and I was still travelling by bus.

I wanted a scooter more than I had ever wanted anything ever before. Except maybe the chocolate machine that I had put on every Christmas list since the age of seven. I could afford to buy one of those now from the money I had put away from the paper round I used to do when I went to school, the summer job I had had the previous year and the money I was getting now from my casual waitressing job. But I didn't because any spare money was going into my scooter fund. I had a few hundred pounds in the Building Society and I thought I only needed a little bit more to be able to buy a Vespa brand new. For the time being though I was stuck on public transport which meant it always took about three times as long to get anywhere as it might have done by scooter.

Finally we arrived at the bus station. I squeezed past the girl at the front, who was chewing on a fingernail and gazing at me gormlessly. She seemed to be staying on for the return journey. I scoured the faces of the people waiting to see if June had got in before me. She had a shock of thick hair that was bleached as yellow as a canary and so was easy to spot amongst the office workers.

June wasn't really a Mod. She made an effort with her clothes but her heart wasn't really in it. She had the pointy shoes, and the black tights, but her skirt was red tartan and her jacket was black leather. At home, she listened to Queen. We had been friends since the first day of college. In one lesson the lecturer had lined us up on one side whilst he talked about seating arrangements. He told us that if we couldn't hear too well we should sit at the front of the class. 'What did he say?' I muttered loud enough to be caught out and made to sit at the front. While I blushed at the risk I'd taken, I saw June laughing and that was that. She was uncomplicated and there was none of the bitchiness in her that seemed to be normal in girls our age.

I walked over to where she was waiting and we linked arms and set off for the Red Cow.

'Are you ready for this, Annie?' she asked.

'I don't know,' I admitted. 'I'm not sure what to expect, are you?'

'Not really, but Ben says there's lots of Mods, lots of scooters, and the music's great.'

'Will Ben be there?' I asked. Ben was June's friend from her village. He was younger than us, barely sixteen, but had been given a Vespa by his elder brother Tom when Tom had passed his test and moved on to a bigger scooter. June had already had an illegal backie off him round the village.

'He said he would be, so at least we'll know someone.'

The Red Cow was well-known as a Mods' venue. We were going there for the 60s Soul Night they held every fortnight. It was a regular pub downstairs but upstairs was a large room with a dance floor that they used for nights like this. There was a huge car park and as we walked up to it we could see perhaps twenty or so scooters parked up in three neat rows.

I gripped June's arm a little tighter. New situations always made me nervous and I would never have had the courage to come here on my own. If June was nervous, she didn't show it. She spotted Ben's scooter in the front row and headed straight for it. Ben was crouched on the ground fiddling with a part of the engine. He stood up when he saw us coming.

'You don't have a cloth or anything, do you?' he asked, looking at both of us in turn and showing us his oily fingers.

'I've got a tissue,' pulling it out of the depths of my pocket. He smiled as he took it.

'No snot on it I hope.'

Despite being a scooter rider and therefore fitting my definition of cool, Ben was somehow definitely uncool. Maybe it was his age, or maybe it was his hair which was curly when it should have been sleek, but whatever it was, I didn't fancy him. This was good of course, because it meant I could relax in his company.

June, who was relaxed in anyone's company, had already sat herself down on Ben's scooter.

'Make yourself at home,' he said.

'Thanks, I will,' she answered, putting her feet up on the top of the front panels.

'I like your scooter,' I said, more as something to say rather than because I actually admired it. It was a very ordinary 50 Special, but a bit too Mod-ed up for me – a few too many lights and mirrors. I preferred them without the accessories. There were plenty of different styles here in the car park though. Not everyone wanted their scooter to look like it came from the sixties.

'Is your brother here?' I asked.

'Not yet. He said he might be along later.'

Much later, I hoped. Tom was very different to Ben. Three years older, he had a job working for a local paper and so could afford sharp suits and refinements to his Lambretta. I had come across him a couple of times when visiting June, hanging out at the bus stop, but he had never spoken to me and so, of course, I had never spoken to him.

More and more scooters arrived, some singly, others in twos or threes. The sound of a scooter engine is very distinctive. It ranges from the excitable squeal at full throttle to the eager turnover at idling speed. It is rough and unrefined but always insistent and keen. If it were a person, I thought, a scooter would run errands for its dear old Nan. It would be quite likely found throwing up into a gutter in the early hours of Saturday morning but would then spend the next twenty minutes trying to find some way of sluicing the vomit away.

The scooter sounds both relaxed me and cheered me up. I was beginning to feel as if I belonged here a little. I took a couple of steps backwards, feeling for something to lean on. My bottom found something just as my calves hit a strip of metal. Whatever was behind me gave way too easily, it leapt away from me as if it was scared of me. I hit the ground as Ben realised what was happening and made a lunge for the object behind me. It was a scooter of course. There was a scrape of metal on tarmac before he managed to right it again. There was a lot of commotion but out of the noise came the thud of army boots and an 'Oi!' as someone grabbed my arm and pulled me to my feet.

'Bloody females,' the person said, 'who lets them in here?' He glared at me and then moved to examine the damage to his scooter. It was an old thing, as big as a tank compared to some of the newer models and in need of some restoration. I managed a 'Sorry' but the owner wasn't listening. Having established that none of the scratches and dents on it could definitely be attributed to me, he glared at me once again.

'Respect the machine,' he declared, describing a wide exclusion zone around the scooter with his hands, before stomping back to a small group in the middle of the car park.

My companions had been struck as dumb as me. Ben obviously felt responsible but also embarrassed for me.

'Blimey,' he said, 'you don't want to get on the wrong side of him.' I looked over to the scooter owner. He was square-faced and sandy-haired and was dressed head to foot in Army Green. He looked older than us, maybe even mid-twenties. He and his friends were all looking over in my direction and scowling. Ben was right, I clearly didn't want to make an enemy of this group.

'Who is he?' June asked, buoyed up with the excitement of events.

'That's Lance,' replied Ben, 'one of the members of the SeaDogs S.C.'. I had heard of the SeaDogs. They were a scooter club that had been going for a few years, before becoming a Mod had become fashionable again. Its members were all in their twenties and didn't seem interested in admitting any new, younger members. Their status made them people to look up to and respect, so I was going to have to hope they forgot about this incident pretty quickly or I was going to find myself bit of an outcast.

'Why do they call themselves the SeaDogs?' June continued, 'there's no sea here.'

'Oh, well, Lance's nickname is Salty, isn't it,' said Ben, as if that explained everything. 'Don't *you* call him Salty though,' he went on, looking pointedly at both June and me. I wasn't bloody likely to call him anything, except maybe 'Sir' for a bit. Actually I was relieved that we weren't allowed to use his nickname. I always felt uncomfortable calling people I didn't know very well by familiar names. One of the day-release boys at college had introduced himself as 'Ax, short for Axle.' His real name was Paul but no one called him that. June wasn't inhibited like me and she would happily get his attention by yelling 'Hey, Ax!' across the canteen. If I wanted to get his attention, I would have to go up and tap him on the shoulder or just shout 'Hey,' in his general direction and hope that he would be one of the people who responded to my shout.

I glanced back over to Lance and his mates again. They seemed to have forgotten about me and were instead gathered around a newly arrived scooter and discussing its features. I still felt uncomfortable though. I felt silly in my parka. I took it off and wrapped it up until I was holding it in a big bundle in front of me. It was more comforting that way, like a soft toy or a pillow.

June noticed my discomfort. 'Shall we go in?' she asked. I nodded, still not trusting myself to be able to speak.

'I'll see you in there,' said Ben. I thought he was a bit embarrassed about choosing to save the scooter instead of me, although he didn't apologise.

June and I went upstairs. The room was large, very dark and already crowded. Coats seemed to have their own corner so I dumped mine in the pile and we made our way to the bar. Although I didn't look my age and had trouble getting into cinemas I never seemed to have trouble buying a drink. Occasionally some officious bar person would ask me my age, but as long as I looked convincing when I told them I was eighteen (and took a year off my birth date if they asked for that) they usually served me.

Half a lager top later I was feeling a bit more relaxed. We had staked out a little spot by the dance floor and I became immersed in watching the dancing. The music was a revelation to me. I had got excited about Two Tone, and more recently had concentrated on collecting the Mod standards by groups like The Who and Secret Affair, but this Northern Soul, as they called it, was something else. Much of it was held together by a big brass section playing the same rhythm throughout providing the dancers a bass line to dance to. One top of this though was an energetic lead line and singing, mostly about love of one sort or another. There was female singing similar to the Supremes or the Vandellas, and male solo singing.

The DJ was playing a tune in which the singer was singing about Skiing in the Snow which didn't seem to fit with the idea I had that soul music came out of big American cities. This didn't faze the dancers though. Unlike most discos I had been to there were as many, if not more, male dancers on the floor as there were female. Everyone seemed lost in their own world, most looking down towards the floor, but not really seeing, instead concentrating on their moves. Feet movement was the key. Some were making a sort of figure of eight shape with each foot dropping behind the other in turn. I tried it slowly step by step, hoping I could remember it later so I could practice in my bedroom. June saw me and grinned.

'Come on, shall we try it?' she asked, pointing towards the dance floor. I shook my head. My bottom felt sore from the fall in the car park. This dancing was something I wanted to be ready for and I had had enough of showing myself up in public for one night.

'You don't mind if I do though?'

'No, of course not.'

June stepped onto the floor and found herself an empty space. Seamlessly she began moving to the rhythm. Her movements looked so effortless I began to wonder if she had soul records hidden away that she exchanged the Queen tape for as soon as I left her house. I watched her closely in case she started miming along to the words. She looked to be so enjoying herself, if it wasn't such an individualistic dance style I would have been tempted to join her. As it was, I just stood, rather awkwardly, on my own nursing my half empty pint glass.

'Do you think they're singing about the dancers or the moves they're making?'

'Sorry, . . what?' I looked to see who was talking. I had to look down a bit as it was Ben, who was a couple of inches shorter than me. He was stretching towards me so he could be heard above the music. Perhaps that was why I didn't fancy him, he was too eager to please and it was only the unattainable ones that I was drawn to.

'The song, Cool Jerks, is it the people, or the moves?'

'Oh.' I laughed. I saw that Tom had arrived. He and Ben were clearly brothers. They shared the same sharp jaw and eyes with lower eyelids so straight they looked as though they were underlined, although Tom's were a deep brown that made him look as though he hadn't got any pupils, where Ben's were green like mine. Tom was talking to some of Lance's friends who I had seen in the car park earlier.

'Is Tom a SeaDog?' I asked Ben.

'No, he hangs around with them, but they haven't invited him to join, it takes a lot to become a member of that club. They're not Mods you know, they're scooter boys. Tom's a Mod, he hangs around with a group from Southend.'

'Are there any female members?'

'Of the SeaDogs?' Ben snorted with laughter at this.

'What do you mean? Why not?' I asked, affronted.

'Well, all sorts of reasons. Scooter clubs are mostly about the scooters. Girls might ride them, but they're not very interested in the mechanics. Then there's the scooter rallies, who wants to have girls trailing behind them at those? Also, suppose you're going out with one and you want to dump her but she's still part of the club, how would that be?'

Ben looked at me as though he was actually expecting an answer to this. I shrugged my shoulders, not knowing how to reply. He carried on:

'See, that girl over there?' he pointed over towards the bar, where I saw a girl who looked like a better version of me, more successful haircut, make-up, clothes, the lot. I nodded.

'Well, that's Sam. She's been going out with Dave,' he pointed over to a tall, friendly-looking bloke in the middle of the SeaDogs group, 'for two years probably, and still she's not allowed to join. She set up her own club in the end. Sessex Girls, they're called.'

'And do they have scooters and go to rallies?'

'Most of them, I think. There's only about five of them. Sam's passed her test and got a

PX200. She knows Tom. She comes round our house sometimes. Once she gave me a lift up here.' Ben was looking over at Sam, longingly.

'Do you think they'd let me join?'

'I wouldn't have thought so, they're more difficult to get into than the SeaDogs.' We were quiet for a while, listening to the music and watching the dancers. Then Ben said, 'You could join mine if you want.'

'Do you belong to a scooter club then?'

'No, but I could start one. We could be the founding members.'

Or only members, more like. I couldn't see the two of us attracting a big following. We might as well call it BenAnnie S.C.. We'd need to make June honorary member to attract the lads and Tom to get the girls in. Still, how many members does it take to make a club? I supposed it might be a laugh.

'OK,' I said to Ben, 'You think of a name and I'll get the t-shirts printed.' We shook hands to seal the deal.

Chapter Two

It was several weeks before I got to go to the Red Cow again. June was busy and I wasn't brave enough to go on my own. I did see a few people I recognised from there in town, often at the motorcycle park in the centre and occasionally one of them would nod to me. I worked a few waitressing sessions and put most of the money away. By the end of February I had £450 in my building society account. This seemed like a huge sum, but actually I didn't know how much a scooter cost.

The nearest place that sold them was Mayling Motorcycles, about 10 miles away. It wasn't in town and since I couldn't get there myself, I bothered Mum until she caved in and agreed to take me. She wasn't overjoyed at the thought of me buying a scooter, but since she had had one in the 1950s, she wasn't really in a position to stop me.

I knew how to get round her: get the photo album out of her scooter trips and get her to talk about them. There was one of a big group of girls and boys somewhere on the coast, all with their helmets and gloves, all stuffing their faces with ice cream. Mum was stood at one side. She was wearing a suede jacket and a billowing flowery skirt. She looked no older than me.

'So, you used to belong to a scooter club, then?' I asked her.

'Yes, we used to go out for day trips together. That one was to Scarborough, I think,' she replied.

'Did you fancy any of the blokes?' I examined the picture to see who I thought was most appealing. There was a chap at the back who had a nice smile.

'I don't think so, they were all a bit older than me. I was only seventeen. In my day we had to get married if we wanted to have a proper relationship with someone. It wasn't like it is now, you know. We couldn't try them out like you lot do. You had to choose very carefully, because you'd be stuck with them for life.'

I had heard this many, many times. Despite Mum's outward disapproval of the freedom of relationships, underneath I thought she was quite jealous. It was also a subtle invitation for me to tell her about my own exploits. Not that I was going to, ever. Quite apart from the embarrassment of discussing such things with my Mum, apart from a couple of fumbled snogs at a party after we'd finished our O Levels, I had nothing at all to tell her about.

I pointed to the boy at the back of the group. 'What about him though, he looks nice.' I said.

Mum looked at the photo. 'Yes, and I think he was already married, or engaged at least. Anyway scooters were for people who couldn't afford cars. You really wanted to set your sights at someone who earned a bit more.'

'Did Dad have a car when you met him?'

'Well, he had a post office van, not quite the same thing.'

'Car drivers are so boring, though. I'm never going to learn to drive.'

'Yes, well, we'll see,' Mum answered, which was usually how she rounded off conversations. Still, getting her all nostalgic, did mean she was quite keen to have a look at scooters and how they had changed in the intervening twenty five years. Her first statement was that they had hardly changed at all. 'It's like bicycles and sewing machines, they designed them once and despite all the twiddly bits they add on, the basic design's no different from the first one.'

'That's not true,' I replied, 'the first bikes had one big wheel and one tiny one.'

'Yes, well the first ones after they got someone sensible to design them then,' she said.

We continued looking round the shop. There were only a few scooters hidden amongst all the motorbikes.

'Are you sure you don't want a motorbike?' my mum asked. 'This one looks nice', she continued, pointing to a Yamaha.

'No Mum! You're missing the whole point. If I had one of those I would have to hang out with the fizzy boys.'

'The who?'

'The fizzy boys.' I pointed to the lettering on the side of the bike. 'Look – F S 1 E – fizzy'.

27

'Oh. And are they not nice boys?'

'No,' I said. 'Wrong attitude'.

I steered Mum back up to the scooters before she got any more silly ideas.

'I don't see any Lambrettas,' she noted.

'No, they don't make them anymore. Not in Italy anyway. You can only get Indian ones, so no one buys them. It's Vespa or nothing.'

'Oh, that's a shame. I had a Lambretta.'

'I know Mum, you've told me. An LD 150 with two seats and sometimes you took Grandma on the back.'

'Yes well I did. She didn't enjoy it much though, I seem to remember. She left me with red patches on my sides where she'd been clinging on so tightly.

We surveyed the range of scooters.

'Do you like any of them then?'

'Well this one, I think,' I replied pointing to a Vespa 100. 'I can ride up to a 125 without doing the test so I could have this PX, but I don't like it much, it's a bit sort of . . . boxy.'

'Anything I can help you with, ladies?' The shop owner had come over.

'Oh, well I was looking at this Vespa 100.'

'They don't make these any more, you know. Discontinued last October. So if you wanted one of these, it would have to be this one.'

This one. I wondered if I was looking at *my* scooter. It was burgundy in colour. It had no indicators so I was going to have to use my arms like on a bike. Despite this, I liked it. It was quite small and stream-lined. It looked like a good match.

'Do you want me to pull it out for you? There's no petrol in it so you can't have a test ride.'

I nodded relieved that I wasn't going to show myself up by not knowing how to ride it. The owner pulled the scooter into the aisle and I sat on it and experimented with pushing it off the stand and pulling it back up again. Off the stand I could get both feet down on the ground at the same time. It seemed quite light and controllable. I knew I wanted it, even though I was slightly scared of it. I looked at the price tag attached to the frame. I could just about afford it outright, although I'd need to borrow money from my parents for a crash helmet and insurance.

'I like it,' I said to my Mum.

'Me too,' she said, 'can I have a sit on it?'

I moved off it to let her have a try. I thought it was important to get her excited about it too.

'Do you want to have a think about it?' she asked.

'You could, but I can't hold it for you without a deposit,' interjected the shop owner.

I looked hopefully at Mum.

'Well . . . if you want it . . .'

'I do.'

'We'd better sort out the deposit then,' she said. I gave her a hug.

For the next few days I was alternately excited and anxious. Mum had written a cheque for the scooter, we had picked out a helmet and gloves and sorted out the insurance and I had arranged to repay her from my building society account. Everything was place for the scooter to be picked up the next weekend. I wasn't sure how I was going to get it back though. The shop didn't seem to do deliveries.

'You'll have to ride it back,' was Mum's fairly obvious solution.

'But I don't know how to!' I said. 'And I'll have all that traffic and roads to deal with too. It'd be much easier to learn here.'

Mum thought about it for a bit. 'I'll pick it up for you then,' she offered eventually.

'Do you remember how?'

'Of course,' she replied airily. It's like falling off a bike.'

And so the following Saturday she took herself off on the bus and I waited anxiously at home for her return. She seemed to take ages. Dad had returned from his post round before she showed up. I had the kitchen window open to listen out for the tell-tale sounds of the engine and as soon as I heard it I was out of the door to see her arrive.

'How did you get on?' I asked as she removed my gloves and my helmet. I was a little jealous that she had ridden my scooter before me.

'Yes, fine. I need a cup of coffee though, it's not like it was in my day, far too much traffic and no one gives you an inch. You're going to have to be careful.'

Dad came out to look the scooter over. He fiddled about with it a bit.

'Go on then,' he said, 'your turn.'

The moment had arrived. I was going to have to ride it. I took the helmet from Mum and put it on. My sister, Julia, came out to watch.

'It looks a bit tinny,' she said.

'Well it is made out of old tin cans and the engine came off a hairdryer,' I retorted before she could get any more insults in. With all of them watching I wanted to look as if I was in control of the machine. I wheeled it round.

'So, what do I do?' I asked Mum.

'Well you need to get it started first. Turn the key, hold the brake in, that's here' she said indicating the lever by one of the handle bars, 'then kick down on this lever here'.

I tried it. The engine coughed.

'Try again, with a bit more welly,' she encouraged.

I did and the engine began to tick over.

'Right now, when you're ready, take it off the stand. You'll need to be in gear, so pull in the clutch, turn it to first then let it out slowly and twist the throttle at the same time.'

It seemed so easy. I pulled in the clutch, turned it to first, let it out and stalled the engine.

'You have to do the throttle too,' Julia said helpfully

'Don't you have something better to do?' I asked her.

'Nope. Anything else is far less fun than this,' she replied.

I put the scooter back on the stand and went through the procedure again. This time I moved off too quickly, panicked and stalled again.

'See?' said my sister looking highly amused.

'Don't listen to her,' said Dad, 'you'll get the hang of it sooner or later. It took you ages to learn how to ride a bike. At one point I thought you would never get to grips with it.'

'And swimming,' he added after the moment.

'Thanks, Dad,' I said, 'you're not helping.'

I had another go. This time I moved off into the middle of the cul-de-sac. It felt great, exciting and scary in equal measures.

'You'll need to change up,' Mum shouted after me. 'Second gear!'

I experimented with that and wobbled off out of the cul-de-sac and down the road. Luckily it was a quiet road and there were no cars coming. I turned another corner in the road. A junction was looming and I needed to brake and stop. I pulled on what I thought was the brake; at least it was where the brake was on my pushbike. Nothing happened. I panicked. Still trying to brake I mounted the kerb, rode across the pavement and a stretch of grass and ended up in someone's hedge. I let go of the controls and the engine cut out.

Feeling foolish, I pulled the scooter out of the shrubbery and looked around furtively to see if anyone was watching. It looked as though I had got away with it. There were a couple of minor scratches on the front mudguard. I couldn't believe it; I had damaged my scooter on its first outing.

I wheeled it over the road and onto the pavement. I decided I had better figure out where all the controls were before I tried again. This time I noticed the brake pedal by my right foot and realised that I had used the other brake when kick starting.

Taking a deep breath, I started the scooter up again. This time I was a little more successful. I managed to make it back up the road and into the cul-de-sac where I braked unevenly and stopped next to Mum who was still waiting on the drive.

'You didn't say about the brakes,' I said accusingly, pulling a leaf out of the gap between my cheek and the helmet.

'Oh, well, they're here and here, she said pointing,' do them both at the same time or you risk flying over the handlebars. It looks as though we'd better get those L plates on quickly, let other drivers know to give you a wide berth.'

I continued to practise on my scooter over the weekend and slowly got more confident on it. On Monday morning I decided to make the journey in to college on it. It was the first time I had encountered anything in the way of traffic and kept close to the kerb as cars and vans overtook me.

When I got near town I took a long cut that avoided a major roundabout and eventually made it to college. I parked up in the motorbike park, still 20 minutes earlier than I would have been if I had come by bus, and waited for June to arrive.

She gave a whoop when she saw me sitting on the scooter and had a good look around it, admiring it.

'Have you got a name for it yet?'

'No. Should I have?'

'Well yes. Is it a he or a she? Most blokes have scoots or cars that are female, but they're male, so . . .'

'So you think mine should be male?'

'Yes. If we can think of a good name for him.'

We agreed to think about it and went into college. It felt good to be carrying my crash helmet, it looked and felt as if I was a proper Mod, or scooter girl as I was now beginning to think of myself. It made the clothing choices wider as I could now dress for comfort rather than style. Still I was thinking of copying the male style of dress although perhaps not with the same emphasis on army surplus. I wished I knew a few other girls with scooters to compare notes.

Later as we worked in the training kitchen, prepping up for lunchtime food service, I stationed myself by the window overlooking the bike park. I had put the lock on so I was confident that my scooter would be safe enough but still I wanted to keep an eye on it. I saw a couple of lads walking by it, stop and give it the once over. I would have done the same, wanting to know who it belonged to. There wasn't too much to admire as was just the basic scooter. I began wondering how I should customise it. Not with lights and mirrors, but with something that made it a bit different.

'Were you planning to let this boil dry?' shouted Mr Creal in my ear, picking up the pan of pears that I had put on to poach, and bringing me rapidly back to the present.

'Are you taking it up to the Red Cow on Wednesday?' June asked later as we perched on the low wall edging the bike park, eating our lunch.

'Will you meet me there if I do?'

'Yeah. Maybe I'll get Tom to give me a lift.'

'Tom! You're not seeing him are you?'

'No. Not *seeing* him as such.'

'Just shagging him then?' June was well known for her casual and uncomplicated sexual relations with boys.

'Well, you know, now and again. There's nothing in it, just 'passing the time' as he says.'

'Oh, he talks as well does he? He's never spoken to me.'

'No, well, I expect he knows you won't put out. Doesn't think it's worth wasting his time.'

'That's a bit unkind.'

'Do you think so? It wasn't meant to be. It's more, well, there's you and there's him,' June represented us as two Wotsits held arms width apart, 'and you're so different there's no point in you trying to get closer 'cos it just wouldn't work. You both like scooters and maybe some of the same music, but that's it, end of similarity.' She placed both Wotsits under her upper lip giving her orange fangs, before scooping them into her mouth with her tongue. I giggled.

35

'In fact,' she said, digging into my crisp packet, 'you're so different, he's a Wotsit and you're a Hula Hoop.' She held these up and experimented with trying to slide the Wotsit into the Hula Hoop. 'See?' she said. 'They don't go.'

'I suppose'

'You'd never cope with a casual shag. You'd be wanting him to send you flowers or something afterwards.'

'No I wouldn't.'

'You would. You'd be complaining 'cos he hadn't phoned. You need someone a bit more thoughtful.'

'Or just someone. Maybe I'm not that fussy.'

'You are. That's why you don't have anyone 'cos you have this look of 'don't touch me' so no one bothers to ask. It's like getting the scooter. Blokes want to be a bit in charge, so they might say, 'let me take you out tonight, I'll pick you up' and you'll say 'It's okay, I've got my scooter, I'll make my own way'. It's too much for them.'

'Oh.'

June had put me right off my sandwich, which was corned beef anyway. I unwrapped my Club biscuit.

'So why do you and I get on then? We don't have much in common.'

'Ah well, one, we're not looking to have sex with each other. Well you're not looking to have sex with me anyway.'

I gave her a Paddington hard stare.

'Joke. And two, we each understand the other person and we still think they're okay. I might think you're mad to spend £500 on a scooter, but if that's what you want to do, I say go ahead and do it. You might think meeting up with someone just for a shag is against your principles but you don't think any less of me for it.'

'Sounds reasonable.'

'Yeah. I should be doing psychology not catering. Also, we both laugh at the same things and that's probably most important of all. Tom, I can exclusively reveal has no sense of humour whatsoever.'

'Hmm, so how am I going to find a bloke if I'm so stand-offish?'

'You don't need one now. You've got Luigi.'

'Luigi?'

'Yeah, that's the name I've chosen for your scooter. He is Italian, isn't he'

I nodded 'Luigi. I like it.'

I got up to stroke the scooter's headlight casing.

'Buongiorno, Luigi.' I said.

Chapter Three

I tried to time my arrival at the Red Cow so that June was already there but I couldn't see her anywhere as I rode up. Ben was there though so I pulled up next to his scooter.

'Wow,' he said, looking over the scooter. 'June said you'd bought yourself one, how are you getting on with it?'

'Not bad. I've got the hang of how to ride it I think, but I'm still scared being in all that traffic.'

'Yeah. You know, if you do training for your test, they tell you to ride in the middle of the road near the white lines, not on the edge.'

'Do you do that?'

'I do now. Makes all the difference, other drivers have to think more about overtaking you so they can't squeeze you into the gutter.'

'I might try that then. Have you seen June anywhere?'

'I saw her in the village as I was leaving, but I haven't seen her up here yet.'

'Oh, well. I'll wait for a bit.'

We waited in the car park for twenty minutes or so. More scooters arrived until there were about thirty lined up facing the pub. I could see the SeaDogs, but luckily they were over in the far corner so I was well out of their way. Sam and the other girls were grouped near them. I wanted to have a look at their scooters, get some ideas for mine perhaps. I thought about what June had said about me being unapproachable. I didn't think I was like that really but I knew that I didn't come across to people as being friendly. Mostly I was just too scared. What if I went over there and they blanked me? Ben knew Sam, maybe he'd come over with me and introduce me. I turned to him to ask him but he looked like he was making moves to go inside.

'I'm going in,' he said. 'Are you coming?'

I thought I might, but also I'd agreed to meet June in the car park.

'I think I'll wait here a little longer. Maybe see you in there?'

'Yeah, okay. You know where I'll be, hovering on the edge of the dance floor.'

I stayed where I was, sitting on my scooter. It did feel good to be doing this. I tried to look relaxed as if this was a habit for me, to sit on my own in a car park full of scooters. Most of the groups headed inside. It was a clear night and even with the street lights above me, I could see a few stars in the sky. I craned my head back to see if I could make out any constellations.

There was a sudden engine noise behind me. I twisted round to see if it was June and Tom and nearly fell off the scooter in the process.

It wasn't June, or Tom. Whoever it was had a nice scooter though. It looked like one from the sixties, painted in a classic cream and red. The rider parked up along from me and took off his helmet. He ran his fingers through his dark hair, messing it up. Now I could see that it was Dave, one of the SeaDogs who Ben had pointed out to me a few weeks ago. I tried to look inconspicuous, although out of all of the SeaDogs he looked the friendliest. He came between the row of scooters but instead of walking past me, he stopped.

'New scooter?' he asked

'Yes.' I managed, and then trying to be less stand-offish, 'is it obvious?'

'No,' he laughed, 'only I've never seen you or it here before. Although, hold on,' he looked at me closely, 'weren't you the one who knocked Salty's scoot over the other week?'

'Yes, that was me.' I couldn't believe it, an actual conversation with a scooter boy and a SeaDog at that. June would never believe me. 'It wasn't on purpose though.'

'No. I don't think we thought it was. You'd have been in trouble if it was though. That was his Dad's scooter and he's very attached to it, sentimentally, you know. What's your name?'

'Annie.'

'I'm Dave, not David, no one calls me that, not even my Mum,' he said holding out his hand. I gave it shake.

'Are you taking it to Morecambe?' he asked

'Morecambe?'

'Yes, you know the Easter scooter rally.'

'Oh I don't know. It might be a bit far.' I didn't know where Morecambe was, but it sounded far.

'Yeah, maybe wait until Yarmouth?'

'Yes, maybe.'

'Well, I expect they're waiting for me.' He said indicating towards the Red Cow, 'see you inside?'

I nodded, 'Yes, maybe.'

I watched his retreating back. As he left in one direction, June appeared from the other, on foot.

'Who was that? Were you talking to him?'

'Yes. Am I allowed?'

'Allowed? You're positively encouraged. Now, who was it?'

'Dave. SeaDog Dave.'

'Wow. I'm impressed'

'Anyway never mind that now. What happened to you? Where's Tom?'

'Oh, you'll never guess. We got pulled over. By the coppers. They wanted to see his documents. Turns out he hasn't passed his test after all, so I was riding illegally. They don't know that yet. He's got a five day wonder so he'll have to take his papers in and they'll find out then probably. Don't know what will happen, he might lose his licence. They've got my name too. Anyway they let him drive on but he said he probably shouldn't take me any further so I had to wait for a bus.'

'Blimey. Did he even take his test?'

'I think he took it but failed. I don't know what on. But he didn't want to lose face so he said he'd passed and moved on to the Lambretta anyway. That's the thing that'll really get them, he'd be okay if he was just riding a 50cc without L plates, but riding a bike he's not legally allowed to drive, they won't like at all.'

41

'What about you?'

'Well I'll just have to hope they believe me when I tell them I thought he had passed his test. There's no point in worrying about it. Shall we go in?'

We wandered over to the pub entrance where we could hear the music pounding joyfully inside. June's news had upset me a bit but I was still elated over having spoken to Dave and I wanted to get in there and celebrate. It'd have to be on lemonade though since I was driving home.

We went in and dumped our coats. Ben immediately spotted us and came over to see what had kept June. I could see she didn't want to tell him what had happened and she kept saying 'Ask Tom. You'll have to ask Tom' until eventually he got his coat and left. He looked worried and I thought they were perhaps making too much of it. No one was hurt or anything, Tom had just got caught out in some stupid lie.

I bought drinks for June and I and we found a spot along a wall near the dance floor. We had to talk quite loudly over the music.

'I'm going to join you this time,' I shouted in her ear.

'Dancing?' she asked. I nodded. I had been practising at home. There was quite a good record shop in town and it had a small Northern Soul section. I had bought a red vinyl disc that had Gloria Jones singing Tainted Love on one side, a song I knew well from the Soft Cell version and a number of tracks by different artists that I didn't know on the other. After college, if Mum was out, I had been putting it on and practising dancing to it in my bedroom. I was quite confident that I'd got my legs moving in the right rhythm but I wasn't sure about my arms. I would have to have another look to see what everyone else was doing.

'Come on then,' June said, grabbing my arm. We put down our drinks and headed for an empty spot in one corner of the floor. It took me a moment to get going, but I soon got in the swing of it and after a while I was concentrating on my own enjoyment rather than looking around to see what everyone else was doing. I had on a pair of white boxing boots that I had bought to wear on the scooter and they were soft and flexible, allowing me to lift my heels while keeping the ball of my foot on the ground and make, I hoped, a few clever foot movements.

I was so lost in the music that I jumped when someone tapped me on the shoulder. It was June.

'I've got to go. The last bus is due in 10 minutes'

'Oh, okay, I'll come out too.'

We went to finish our drinks, although they had gone flat in the time we were dancing. I saw Dave coming over.

'That looked like fun.'

'It was.' I replied.

'You should have joined us,' said June, pulling on her coat.

'Maybe another time,' he replied.

'He likes you!' exclaimed June in a loud whisper in my ear as we went down the stairs. She seemed to be excited for me.

'He's got a girlfriend,' I replied, although I was excited too and this seemed like a small obstacle.

'Don't let that stop you,' said June, heading for the bus station. 'See you tomorrow.'

'Yeah, see you.'

I drove home, happily, exuberantly. I even braved the big roundabout which didn't seem too scary at 10.30 at night. The roads were quite empty and I took Ben's advice in driving in the middle of the road. I felt free, as if I could do and achieve anything. Since there was no one to hear me, I began singing loudly.

I thought about Dave and remembered what he had said about the scooter rallies. I had heard of them, of course. All those Mods in Brighton that time must have been on a scooter rally. Now I had a scooter, I could go on one. I could be part of that sea of khaki and shiny paintwork lined up on the sea front. I wondered where Morecambe was. Maybe, I thought, I had better find out.

Chapter Four

I still owed Mum for the extra she had put in for the scooter and recently seemed to have been spending much more quickly than I had been earning. One thing was for certain, if I wanted to go on rallies I was going to need some money. Last summer I had worked in a factory picking out bits of shells from walnut pieces as they bounced past on a conveyor belt. That's when I had saved most of the money for the scooter. Since then I'd signed up with an outside catering company doing waitressing at big dos like weddings and business functions. It had all gone a bit quiet since Christmas though. I decided to give them a ring to see if they had any work available. It turned out that one of their regular staff members had gone sick and so they fitted me in for a shift the following weekend.

So Saturday night found me sitting in the back of a minibus with the other waitresses heading for a big hall somewhere out on the marshes.

'Do you know what sort of a do this is?' I asked Maureen, one of the regulars who was sat next to me.

'A late Christmas bash, I think. Or early Easter. Who knows?' she replied. 'It's for Crendell's.' Crendell's was a soft drinks company in town. 'If it's for the whole staff there'll be hundreds of them. My nephew works there and he's going.'

I didn't enjoy this work much. It was hard on your feet and tiring but it paid relatively well for a waitressing job. We were all allocated our own table with about twenty people on it. Usually with these things it was a set menu so unless you had a vegetarian or someone had a complaint, or they were bored with the company on their table you hardly spoke to any of the guests.

I had a table right at the far end of the hall meaning I had the furthest to go from the kitchens. I was glad I had comfy shoes on. I finished setting up the cutlery and glasses in double quick time and helped the girl on the table next to me, then we all went to sit down to eat before the guests arrived.

The hall when it was full was a completely different scene from when it was empty. Clearly this was an important celebration as everyone was dressed up, the men in suits and the women in party dresses. Most of the men didn't look as if they were used to wearing a suit, some of them were fiddling with shirt collars or ties and many didn't seem to know what to with their hands.

There was an MC who began the proceedings and everyone moved to their seats. This was our cue to begin service. Starters were easy since they were cold and you could fit four of them up your arm, so you only had to make five trips instead of the ten for the main course. In the kitchen there was a mad grab for the plates and the chefs struggled to keep up with our speed of service. I was convinced they had the easier job though.

On my second trip out of the kitchen I thought I saw a face I knew on one of the tables over on the right. It was a man, but I couldn't quite place him. Needing to concentrate on balancing my plates I decided to have another look once I'd got the entire table out.

But then I forgot and was kept busy with clearing plates and getting the next course out. It was beef bourguignon and it smelt great. To begin with the service seemed to be going pretty smoothly. But then there was a huge crash in the middle of the room. A cheer went up around the room as was usual in these instances.

Having delivered my plates I went over to see if I could do anything to help. It was Maureen. She had just cleared her last stack of starter plates and had caught her foot in a carelessly stowed bag handle. The plates and cutlery had gone flying and Maureen herself had landed on her knees. One of the other waitresses helped Maureen out of the hall and I got down on the floor to pick up the broken plates.

Once the initial excitement was over of course the guests just wanted their food. We now all had to work a bit harder and faster so that we could cover Maureen's table too. By the time I remembered there was someone I was going to check out we were on to coffees. Finally, having poured the last cup, I had a moment to catch my breath. Most of the guests had lit up cigarettes by then and it was quite difficult to see through the haze. I had even forgotten where I had seen the man I thought I recognised. Finally I spotted him again. For a moment I still couldn't place him. Then I realised that it was Lance. Dressed up in a suit he looked almost unrecognisable. He looked as though he was having a good time. He actually had a smile on his face and was talking animatedly to the person opposite him.

I felt a little jolt when I realised that the person that he was talking to was Dave. I hadn't known that they both worked at Crendell's, but then why would I? In truth I didn't know anything about either of them.

I began closing in on their table on the pretext of looking for stray plates and empty bottles to collect. I saw that Sam was sat next to Dave. Maybe she worked there too. Or maybe they had brought partners. I wondered who Lance might have brought. He had a woman either side of him but they both looked middle aged. Sam looked sleek and elegant in a midnight blue dress. I felt deeply envious of her ability to look right and also of her place at Dave's side. I had reached the table and was facing Dave. I decided to be bold.

'Excuse me, are these finished with?' I asked, leaning into the centre of the table and indicating some wine bottles.

'I don't know. Are they?' Dave asked, more to himself than to me. He lifted up one of the Mateus Rose bottles.

'Yeah, we drained them,' said Sam.

Dave passed them up and in doing so, actually looked at me. 'Oh, hello,' he said, surprised.

I smiled. 'Hello,' I said, 'having a good time?'

'Yeah, great, thanks,' Dave replied. 'Nice food. Compliments to the chef and all that.'

I was standing at Lance's shoulder. He looked up but there was no sign of recognition on his face.

'This is Annie,' explained Dave. 'She comes to the Red Cow sometimes. Just bought herself a scooter, haven't you?'

I was grateful that he hadn't reminded Lance that I was the one who had knocked his scooter over.

'What've you got?' asked Sam, looking me up and down.

'Oh, a Vespa 100.'

'Small frame?' I nodded. 'Nice scoot, I used to have a Primavera.'

'A 125?'

'The same. It's good to see more girls into scooters,' she added.

'That wasn't you earlier was it? Broke all those plates?' This was Lance; perhaps he had recognised me.

'No, that was Maureen,' I said, just as one of the wine bottles slipped from my grasp. Lance caught it and passed it back up to me.

'Maureen? Is she okay?'

'Yes, she's fine, embarrassed mostly.'

'Good. Be careful on that scooter then won't you?' he said.

'Yes, better get on,' I mumbled. 'Enjoy the rest of your evening.'

On the minibus on the way back I sat next to Maureen again. She had plasters on both knees but seemed okay otherwise.

'Did you see your nephew then?' I asked her

'I saw him, but didn't speak to him. I didn't get the chance.'

'What does he do at Crendell's?'

'He's a forklift driver in the warehouse. He showed me round one time, you know. It's fascinating, like one of those programmes of factories you see on the telly. There's a constant stream of bottles lining up to be filled with whatever drink they've got on the line at that time, then they're all capped and lined up to be picked off to go in the boxes. They take in returned bottles too so they have to clean and sterilize them first. Some people have the job of making sure these are empty before they go through the sterilizer and you'd never believe what they find in them sometimes.'

'What sort of things?'

'Well crisp packets and fag packets, that's normal, you can imagine some people bored in a pub rolling up their rubbish to squeeze it through the neck, can't you. They're always impossible to get out, Lance says. But the worst are rats and mice.' She shivered.

I was suddenly interested. 'Did you say Lance?'

She nodded.

'Does he ride a scooter?'

'Oh yes. Do you know him?

'Sort of. I knocked over his scooter one time.'

'Oh he wouldn't have liked that. He's been into them since he was a nipper. Got the bug off his dad, my brother,' she explained. 'He was a proper Mod, my brother. Got his picture in the paper when they had that ruckus up at Clacton one bank holiday. Marie, Lance's mother wasn't too happy about it. He used to leave her at home alone looking after the baby.'

'Lance?'

'Yes. Odd name, isn't it? Apparently he was named after some soul singer. Major Lance or something.'

Maureen could talk for England once she got going so I learned all sorts of things about Lance that probably he would not have wanted me to know. About how his Dad got off with some girl on a run out to the coast when Lance was still young. About how his Mum found out and chucked him out and he went up North to live with this new woman. About how young Lance used to be driven up halfway up to Manchester once a year by one of his family members down south to some spot where they used to meet up with his Dad so he could have his visitation rights.

'Lance blamed his step-mum for breaking up his family, you know, not his Dad. He's got a thing against women somehow as a result. That's my view anyway. Never had a girlfriend, you know. At least not as far as I know. That's not right is it?'

'No. That's not right.' I agreed.

'He's twenty-one, he should be sowing his wild oats while he's got the chance.'

I wasn't sure I agreed with Maureen on that point, but I didn't say so.

Chapter Five

The end of term was approaching at college. We had a few tests but nothing too difficult. Accommodation science was focussing on cleaning floors and we had a bit of fun with some industrial buffers. My thoughts though were firmly fixed on Morecambe. I had looked it up in Dad's road atlas so now knew where it was. It was a very long way away, about three hundred miles, I thought. I couldn't really see me doing it on my scooter, it would take all day. But that didn't stop me daydreaming about going.

I had worked a couple more sessions with the outside caterers and Mum had started giving me the family allowance again now that she considered my debt repaid. So I had a bit of money in my pocket. Realistically, Morecambe probably wasn't an option, but maybe I could plan for Yarmouth.

Then, the week before Easter when we had broken up from college and I was in the garden with the Turtle Wax polishing the scooter, I got a phone call. It was June.

'How much do you want to go to Morecambe?'

'Lots. Why?'

'Cos I've got us a lift, that's why.'

'On a scooter?'

53

'No, in a car, dumbbell. I know it's not how you're supposed to get there but it's better than not going, surely? And we can both go.'

'Oh, well then, yes, let's go. Whose car though?'

'Salty's.'

'Lance, you mean. Since when have you known him? You're not shagging him now are you?'

'No, course not.' No, I hadn't thought it was likely really.

'No. I don't know him at all. It wasn't him who asked us. Turns out Dave, your Dave, has broken his arm somehow so he can't ride up and Lance's scooter probably isn't in a fit state to get up there anyway, so they decided to drive up. Then they were looking for extra people to fill the car to share the petrol costs. All the other SeaDogs are riding up there and so are the girls so they asked Tom. But he's already arranged to go down to the Mod rally in Margate, so he told Ben about it and he told me.'

'Is Ben planning to come then?'

'Yes, so that's the five of us.'

'Do Dave and Lance know that it is us going with them?'

'I doubt it, since I've only just heard about it and only just asked you.'

'Do you think they'll mind?'

'Mind what?'

'Taking two girls along?'

'Why should they mind if we're paying our way?

'I don't know. I don't suppose Dave will mind, but Lance might.' I hadn't told June what I had heard about Lance, it didn't seem right.

'Oh well, I'll tell Ben we say yes, he can get back to the boys and if they've got any complaints they can let us know, can't they.'

'Okay, but for the meantime, we're going.'

'Yup. Crappy seaside resort on the North West coast filled with thousands of scooter boys, here we come.'

'Indeed. Do you know how Dave broke his arm?'

'Falling off a trampoline, I think.'

'What? Really?'

'No, I don't know actually. I never thought to ask.'

Mum wasn't too keen on the idea of the trip to Morecambe and neither was Dad.

'We don't know either of these boys,' he argued.

'No, but you know June.' He had met her a couple of times but hadn't been over-impressed. I think he thought she was a bit irresponsible, even though she'd been on her best behaviour.

Still, neither of them were the type to lay down the law and I promised to behave myself, leaving it as vague as I could to what that meant in practice. Mum and Dad were worried that we hadn't got anywhere to stay, so we pulled Dad's old ridge tent down from the loft along with a sleeping bag. Mum and Dad seemed a little out of sorts. We had often gone away as a family over the Easter weekend as we had that year in Brighton. But this year Julia had been invited to a wedding and with me now going away as well, they didn't seem to know what to do with themselves.

June phoned again to say that it was all on and to meet her at the Red Cow on Saturday morning. It was a bit of a struggle getting on the bus with all my gear but it proved useful as a something to sit on while I waited by the pub for the others to arrive. It felt as if I was leaving home. I thought about sticking my thumb out at passing traffic and seeing where I ended up. The local DIY merchants probably, as it was an Easter Saturday morning. Either that, or dead in a ditch.

June and Ben showed up. June had a fancy sleeping bag that packed down to the size of a small cushion and a back pack full of make-up and underwear. Ben just had a toothbrush in the pocket of his shirt.

'It's going to be a warm weekend I heard,' he said. 'I've got a few layers on, I'll just shed them as I go.'

He was right, it did seem warm for April. I had worn my parka but already it felt heavy and uncomfortable.

'But what about sleeping?' I asked him.

'There'll be all-nighters, won't there,' he answered. 'I'm not planning on sleeping. I can always kip in the car on the way home.'

The pub was open, hoping for a few early customers and we were just wondering about whether to go in and get a drink when a Ford Granada pulled up in the car park. It had crossed my mind that Lance might've decided to go without us, but, no, there he was with Dave in the passenger seat. They both got out. Lance looked at us a little apprehensively.

'Kids,' he said. 'Kids and girls.' He sighed. 'Oh well. Here's the rules. One: I am not responsible for you. Two: we split the petrol costs five ways. Three: we leave when I say it is time to leave. Four: I am not responsible for you. Got it?' We nodded. 'Right, let's get your stuff in the boot.'

I was surprised to see that they didn't seem to have a tent themselves.'

So was June. 'Aren't you camping?' she asked.

'No, we've got digs. A B&B,' said Dave. 'I'm meeting Sam up there.' Well that made that clear.

'Are you meeting your girlfriend up there, Salty?' June asked, piling in with the questions I would never ask.

'No, he's sharing with Perry,' said Dave. 'Who's not his girlfriend,' he added, as if we thought he might be. 'That's not his real name,' he added. 'He just got really drunk on Babycham when he was thirteen. We'll drop you off at the campsite.'

'And arrange when to meet you on Monday,' said Lance. He wanted to be rid of us I thought. I couldn't blame him really.

'It's quite a way until we plan to stop so if anyone needs the toilet they had better go now,' he added. He seemed to think we were all twelve. I was about to protest, but I thought that might make

57

me look as if I actually was about twelve. Anyway I did need the loo so I went into the pub with June and Ben as suggested.

I was the first back out and managed to bag the window seat in the back of the car behind Dave. I was quite looking forward to the journey. I was always enjoyed seeing different towns and villages and houses and imagining how other people lived.

'Are you alright?' Dave asked over his shoulder, 'not been working too hard?'

'I'm fine,' I answered. I felt quite at home with him already. 'What happened to you though?'

'Stupid accident. I fell off a horse.'

'No? Really?' I didn't believe that.

'Really. No one believes me. I don't know why. Don't I look like a horse rider?'

'No, you look like a scooter rider.'

'Well, I hope so. But I could be both couldn't I?'

'I doubt it.'

'No, well you're right. I've never ridden a horse before and I don't suppose I ever will again. I didn't enjoy it much, not being in control and it didn't like me much, as you can see,' he said, holding up his cast. 'Give me a 200cc combustible engine anytime.'

June and Ben had returned to the car and got in with Ben in the middle. We set off.

No one said much for a while. Lance turned on the music. He had a Motown tape in and we listened to Smokey Robinson and Marvin Gaye for a bit.

I cast a few surreptitious glances at Lance. Up close you could see he was only twenty one even though I had originally thought he looked older. He looked tense, hunched over the steering wheel. I thought about his family history. It wasn't fair of me to know all this information about him without him knowing that I knew. At the same time I didn't want to give myself away with an unguarded comment. He would be bound to want to know how I knew and I didn't think he would be very pleased with Maureen if he found out that she had gossiped about him to me.

The Marvelettes came on the tape and June began to sing along, quietly to begin with but then with increasing volume. None of us joined in but June's exuberance broke the ice a little and once the track ended, we all felt more like chatting.

Ben told us that had Tom lost his licence after he had taken his documents in to the Police. He'd only had a provisional anyway and he said that they weren't going to let him have it back for twelve months. June said that two officers had been round to see her and given her a lecture about making sure that the person who gave her a lift was legally entitled to do so.

'So you've got to ask to see their licence then?' I asked.

'I suppose so,' she answered. 'What am I going to say? 'Can I check your credentials please?'

'You might get more than you bargained for,' said Dave.

59

'Tom's really embarrassed about it,' said Ben. 'He said he'd told so many people he was taking his test and that he'd be driving his Lammy by the weekend that he couldn't face telling them he'd failed. He booked another test and he would have taken that by now if he hadn't been banned so he might have been legal by now anyway.'

'What did he fail on, do you know?' Lance asked.

'No, he wouldn't say,' said Ben.

'Well there's a reason he didn't pass and it might've been pretty serious meaning he's unsafe on the roads,' Lance pointed out. 'It's bad enough riding a larger machine, but he certainly shouldn't have been carrying passengers on it.'

'Yeah. Scooters aren't toys,' said Dave at the same time as Lance said the same thing.

'It's his saying,' explained Dave. 'Lance thinks most people shouldn't be allowed out on the road for their own safety.'

'So you probably don't think Annie or I should have one then?' asked Ben.

'No, not really,' Lance said.

'How about if we take our test?'

'How about if you get proper training?'

Lance had a point I thought. I would have to look into this training thing, I thought.

Ben wasn't finished talking about Tom yet. 'So anyway,' he continued, 'Tom's gone on the train to Margate.'

'What's at Margate?' I asked.

'That's where the Mod rally is,' he replied. 'We're going to the National Scooter Rally and he's going to the Mod rally.'

'Yeah, there's all sorts at the Nationals. Mods are the least of it,' Dave said. 'Tom won't like going by train though.'

'How about us though, going to a scooter rally by car. Is that okay?' June asked.

'Not really, but Salty's got a few mates up in the North West. They'd rather see him than not. He'll get a bit of stick off the lads though.'

'What about the rest of us?'

'Well you two are girls so no one really expects you to have a scoot and Ben could be too young. And I've got my cast on so we've all got good reasons,' said Dave. 'Mind you I'm going to have to come up with another reason for having bust my arm. No one's going to believe the real one.'

'It's not the same though,' he continued, 'not having your scoot. You park it on the front, in the row next to your mates' machines and then that's your spot. That's where you hang out. Other people will come up and have a look at your scoot and you can have a chat about it, what you've done with it and so on. Then a group of you'll decide to have a tour up the end of the front and back and a whole pack of you'll cruise along the road. It'll sound like a scooter symphony and everyone'll look and you'll feel so happy you'll just want to wave at them all.' He stopped lost in his thought. 'No,' he said finally, 'it's not the same at all. Thanks for taking us up there though, Salty, going's better than not going.'

We were all silenced by Dave's little speech. It was June who spoke first.

'Is this your car then, Lance?' she asked

'Yes, it is' he replied.

'So you have a scooter and a car? That's a bit greedy isn't it?'

'The scoot's his Dad's really,' said Dave. Lance didn't seem to be able to answer for himself.

Lance mumbled something under his breath.

'You're such a grump, Salty,' exclaimed June.

'Lance, to you,' he muttered.

'See what I mean?' June could seem as if she was really insensitive to other people at times, but often, I thought, she was doing it on purpose. She might wind a person up and get them riled so they revealed something about themselves. She liked getting a reaction, even if it did take a bit of time and effort. If someone was unresponsive to me, I wouldn't know how to get through to them and we'd never get to know each other. Often that was best, I thought. But it was different with Lance, he intrigued me somehow. I couldn't believe he was against all girls just because he didn't get on with his step-mum. There had to be another reason that he didn't have a girlfriend. Perhaps girls terrified him. If so, June was really going to get a few sparks flying one way or another.

She continued to needle him. 'Shall I give you a neck rub?' she asked, putting her hands on his shoulders and beginning to knead.

'No.' he shook her off. 'Look if you don't want to be left at the next bus stop I suggest you stop that right now.'

June sank back into her seat, defeated, but, I was willing to bet, only temporarily.

Ben contorted himself suddenly, trying to reach his back jeans pocket. 'Could you put this tape on?' he asked, passing a cassette forward. Dave put it on and we listened to the Small Faces for a while. Lance turned up the bass and we opened the windows so the air rushed in, in great swirls. We reached the A1 and began to pick up speed, overtaking slower cars and whooping and waving at them as we went past. I wondered when we'd see some scooters. After a while, and only having seen a Puch moped, we pulled into a roadside café.

'This is the lunch stop,' Lance informed us.

We went in and sat down together at a table by the window. June, Ben and I were squashed on one side with me in the middle. The boys all ordered full fry-ups while June and I went for sandwiches.

'So have you been to Morecambe before?' June asked.

'I went last year, on my scoot that time,' Dave said.

'How about you, Lance?'

'The last two years,' he said shortly.

'It's the first run of the season,' Dave said, 'so you've got to go if you can. You've got to see what everyone's been up to over the winter. See who's got new scooters and what they've done to them, that sort of thing.'

'Yeah, and see who's got a non-runner and has had to come by car,' said Lance morosely.

'But if anyone can make a scoot go, it'll be you, eh, Salty?' June asked.

'What makes you say that?' he asked. He seemed to have forgotten to pull her up on the use of his nickname.

'Oh I don't know. I've heard you're good with machinery. Everyone goes to you if something's wrong, don't they?' June was trying flattery now; it seemed to work better than the needling.

'I don't know about that,' said Lance, but he did look quite pleased.

I felt some pressure on the side of my foot. Someone else seemed to want the place where my feet were. I moved them slightly to give whoever it was room. The foot followed mine and kept up the pressure. I looked at both Lance and Dave to see if they were looking for my response but they were both concentrating on their food.

I decided to return the pressure and see if I could read a reaction on either of their faces. I pushed back against the foot gently and then with a little more force. It was returned and our calves came into contact as well. I realised that it must be Dave because of where his leg was. He gave me a little grin to confirm it. I couldn't help feeling a little bit disappointed that it wasn't Lance showing me a bit of under-table attention. That didn't stop me feeling disappointed when Dave took his foot away.

We got back into the car, this time with June in the middle. Once we got going the steady movement and the warmth of the day lulled me and with my head lolling onto June's shoulder, I fell asleep.

Chapter Six

I woke up to find the car was stationary. We appeared to be in a car park, surrounded by trees, some kind of beauty spot perhaps. Dave, Ben and June were all apparently asleep but Lance was gone. I realised that I needed to go to the loo and decided to get out and see if there was one. The car park, however, appeared to contain nothing but a handful of cars.

To my left was a path that led downwards through some trees. I followed it for a short while and then looked for a tree that was wide enough to hide behind. Checking that I wasn't visible from the car park, I did my wee which was a huge relief. As I was doing up my jeans I saw that the trees did not extend far in the other direction and that beyond them was an open space.

I could hear the sound of running water. I decided to explore a little. I didn't think that Lance would go without me, but I did have to hope that he would notice that I wasn't in the car. Taking the chance, I carried on down the path. Soon it opened on to the clearing. Not a clearing, that wasn't descriptive enough, it wasn't clear at all. It was a meadow, I decided, a meadow filled with soft grass and daisies and buttercups and dandelions. All yellow and green and white.

On the other side of the meadow the ground dropped away to some sort of babbling brook. I wandered over to it. The water was shallow and I could see the smooth stones on the bottom. I wanted to take my boots and socks off, roll up my trousers and wriggle my toes in the cool, clear water. I contented myself with crouching down and letting it run through my fingers. I ran my wet hand over my face and neck, dipped my fingers in again and then sucked them dry.

The sunlight shone on the water, creating ever-changing patterns as the leaves from the trees on the opposite bank drifted gently to and fro in the breeze. I turned back towards the meadow. It was such a beautiful scene, I half expected to see some cartoon bunnies and shy fawns, frolicking on the grass or peeping out from behind the tress like in a Disney film.

But no, what I saw was Lance, facing away from me on a fallen log at the far end of the meadow. I had thought that Army Green was supposed to camouflage its wearer but it didn't work here. Lance looked like a dull thumbprint against all the bright natural colour.

At least I knew he hadn't returned to the car. Perhaps I could get my feet wet after all. Usually the seaside was the place for that but I didn't think much paddling went on at a scooter rally. Ice creams and slots – yes, paddling and donkey rides – no.

Keeping an ear out for Lance, I sat down by the stream and unlaced each boot. I pulled off my socks and pulled up my trousers to my knees. They were fitted jeans so it wasn't easy but once they were there, they stayed there.

Gingerly I dipped my toes in, one foot at a time. And then, feeling brave, I stepped on to the largest stone I could see close to the edge. The water rushed around me. My feet looked red and angry from being cooped up in the boots but soon began to turn white at the toes from the chill of the water. I smiled and then giggled, out loud I thought. It's funny what feeling like a kid could do.

Suddenly I felt that I wanted to stay there, not carry on to some overcrowded seaside town filled with packs of lairy lads on noisy machines. I wanted to hold a net in the water to see what I could catch in it. I wanted to sit by the side of the stream eating thick white bread cheese sandwiches out of a paper bag. I wanted to lie down on a blanket in the middle of the meadow, squashing the grass into the shape of me below.

I climbed out of the water and on to the bank, picking up my boots and socks but leaving my trouser legs bunched up around my knees. I looked over at Lance. He didn't seem to have moved. I wondered what to do. My instinct was to go and see if he was okay but I was nervous of his reaction if I did. I decided to go with my instinct rather than my nerves.

I was certain he could hear me as I approached but he didn't turn to see who it was. From the side I could see that his face was red about the eyes and nose. I had second thoughts about checking on him, but it was too late, turning and running in the opposite direction would be worse. But what was I going to say?

The log was quite long and there was space for me to sit down on it without crowding Lance. I took a deep breath and decided on the non-committal conversation opener.

'I've just had a paddle in the stream. It's beautiful here, isn't it?'

He grunted in reply, but it was a response. I ploughed on.

'Sorry, I know it's none of my business, but are you okay?'

Lance didn't answer for so long, I started to think that he wasn't going to. But then he spoke up.

'Yeah, I'm okay. This place has a lot of memories for me, that's all.'

'Oh. Good memories?'

'A bit of both, I suppose.'

Neither of us spoke for a while. Then I decided there was something I wanted to say. 'Sorry,' I began, 'sorry, that you've ended up with us lot on the journey. You don't really want us, do you?'

'Well, no. But it's not that. It's the whole thing. It's a scooter rally. I should be riding, not driving. It's a completely different thing. It's about freedom and about being in your head. There's no silly chatter on a scoot, even if you've got someone with you.'

I couldn't argue with that explanation.

'Also,' he continued, seemingly on a roll now, 'you're girls. On your own. I can't help worrying about you. But I don't need the responsibility.'

'You don't need to worry about us.'

'You say that, but you're very naïve, you especially.'

'I'm not!'

'You are. You think everyone's like you. And they're not. Morecambe's gonna be filled with thousands of lads. There will be girls there, but not many. The ones who have come on scooters will be able to look after themselves and most of the rest of them will be there because their boyfriend's brought them there. So you're gonna stand out. And any bloke who fancies his chances is going to try it on with you. And you'll be so flattered you won't say no. Like you should.'

He looked at me now, for the first time since I'd sat down beside him.

'Oh.' It sounded as though he knew me better than I knew myself. I felt completely deflated.

'I'm not going there to find a boyfriend.'

'I know. And most lads don't go to a rally to find a girlfriend. Doesn't mean they won't take their chances if the opportunity presents itself.'

'And you think I'm too stupid to say no.'

'I didn't say that.'

'No, but that's what you meant.'

'Maybe. I can't quite make you out, you know.'

'How do you mean?'

'Well why did you buy a scooter? What made you want one? See, most people, I can understand. For some, it's the pose. They want people to look at them. They want to stand out from the crowd. Most girls, especially Sam and that lot, are like that. And they're quite happy to admit it. Some blokes are like that too. Ben's one. Most blokes though are interested in the machinery and the buzz you get from riding it and doing it up so it works better. '

'And that's you.'

'Yes. People like me, their scoot's in pieces more often than it's on the road. We might all wear the same sort of clothes but that's because they're practical for scooter riding. And then there's some people who get into the music first and the scooter follows after.'

'And I don't fit into any of those categories?'

'No. I don't think so. You're not looking for anyone to look at you. You're too quiet for that. You haven't got a clue how a scooter works, I'm willing to bet.'

I shook my head. 'Not really, but I can change a spark plug.'

'So could most people. I don't think it's the music either.'

'No, although I do love it.'

'So what is it? You bought your scooter new didn't you? That's a big layout for anyone of your age. And if you're spending your evenings waitressing, I would think that your family isn't rich.'

'No. I saved up for it.'

Lance had put me on the spot now. I wanted to give him an answer, I wanted to explain myself but I wasn't sure what my answer should be.

'Well my mum had a scooter.'

'When you were little?'

I shook my head. 'No, before I was born.'

'So that's not the reason.'

'Perhaps not, but she did make me think it was possible, that it wasn't strictly a bloke thing. Also she couldn't say no when I said I wanted to buy one.'

'Maybe not, but that doesn't explain why you wanted one in the first place.'

There was a scrunching sound behind us. I turned to see Dave coming towards us.

'You should've woken us, mate,' he said to Lance.

Lance shrugged. I thought he'd probably wanted to be on his own. He stood up.

'We should be getting on if we want to be there by evening,' he said and we all returned to the car. Ben and June were still fast asleep. June had fallen over into the gap I'd left and I had to lift her up to get my space back. In a way I was glad they hadn't woken, that they hadn't found out about that beautiful spot, and that Lance and I had managed to have a conversation without June butting in.

As we set off again, I thought about his question. Why did I buy a scooter? Was it from seeing those Mods on the rally in Brighton? I had tried being a Mod, but I wasn't, I was a Modette, a sort of sub-member somehow. I didn't want to be different because I was a girl. Maybe that was it. But was that ever possible?

I didn't know, but Lance's comments suggested that it wasn't. It wasn't that I wanted to be treated as a male, I just didn't want to be disregarded or treated like some sort of sexual object because I was female. One thing was certain, I wasn't going to fulfil Lance's prediction that I was going to say yes to any bloke that asked me. I wouldn't give him any reason for disrespecting me.

Pretty soon, we were driving through built up areas. Dave said we had to get through Manchester. I had never been up this way before. It seemed a bit like a foreign country. The houses we were passing were no nonsense, tall, blank faced, built up to the pavement. Occasionally a building was set back but it only ever had concrete fronting it. There were trees, but no grass, no flowers. I quite liked it, there was something honest about it all, but I imagined that it would look quite forbidding in the rain.

After we had worked our way through what I thought must be the centre we saw smaller, friendlier houses and then, in front of a pub, a group of scooters and their riders. We went past too quickly, but I was sure there were as many girls as boys. They seemed to have a different look to the scooter riders who hung out at the Red Cow but I couldn't quite put my finger on what it was. I had thought that Mods and scooterists were the same everywhere but maybe I was wrong about that. Maybe if I lived up North there wasn't the distinctions between girls and boys like there were in the South. Maybe I would be so confused if I was a Northerner.

73

Chapter Seven

Through the other side of the city we were out into the countryside again. We began to see more and more scooters, sometimes in twos and threes, sometimes strung out one by one over a distance. By the time we got to Morecambe we must have seen several hundred, but that was nothing to the mass of them in the town itself. Lance negotiated his way carefully past every one of them, always making sure to give them enough space.

I had begun to feel excited about being in the middle of all this, being a part of it. I had had a friend at school who had been obsessed with creating memories. Everything interesting or exciting she did, she seemed to do in order to create a memory of it, rather than for the sake of the thing itself. I had always thought that she was a bit odd but this seemed so different, so outside the experience of everyday life, that I couldn't help making a conscious decision to do my best to record it in my mind.

Pretty soon we were driving along a road that seems to have a lot of B&Bs along it. Scooters were lined up along the both sides of the road. Finally there was a bit of space and Lance pulled into it.

'Dave and I will check into our digs,' he said, 'then I'll take you to the campsite. I thought it might be a good idea if you knew where we were, just in case.'

The three of us in the back nodded.

We waited while the two of them went up some steps to a four storey house a bit further up the road. I could see some scooters I recognised from the Red Cow up there. Only Lance returned.

'Right, anyone know where the campsite is?' he asked as he got back in. No one answered.

'I don't even need to go there,' said Ben, 'since I'm not planning on sleeping. You could just drop me off in the town somewhere.'

'Don't you want to stick with us?' asked June.

'Oh, well, maybe,' he replied, 'I just didn't want you to think that I was planning to bunk down with you two.'

'You can if you like,' said June. 'I'm sure there'll be room for a small one. Eh, Annie?'

'At a push, I suppose. You might be useful, I'm not sure I know how to put the tent up.'

Lance sighed.

'Right, let's find this site,' he said. 'It might be in the same place as last year. It can't be that hard, I'll just follow the scooters.'

He did and we found it easily enough.

'Right, I'm leaving you here,' he said. 'Meet me here at 1pm on Monday – all three of you and don't be late.'

He got back in the car and drove away, leaving us standing holding all our kit. Scooters were weaving past us and so we decided to follow them in to the site. We paid our money and begun wandering through tents looking for a suitable spot to put ours up.

There wasn't much free space and we eventually decided on a spot near the back of the site. It was quite quiet and off the main track so we didn't have many passers-by or scooters going past. This was just as well because our attempts to put the tent up were embarrassing and June and Ben nearly came to blows at one point over who was responsible for letting the whole thing collapse on its side for the fourth time.

Finally we did get it upright and able to stay upright on its own and we all lay inside it to test it for space. June suggested that Ben should go top to tail with us but that meant having his socks by our noses so we soon decided that we'd all have to face the same way.

Apart from the tent erection, I hadn't done anything energetic all day, but I still felt tired out and could happily have dozed off there and missed out on the evening's activities. June however was getting her second wind and revving up for whatever entertainment she could find.

'Come on,' she said, 'I need a wee, a hotdog and a mirror in that order. Then we have to find out what's on, where the music is and all that.'

Ben said that he only needed the hotdog and would see us later, perhaps by the hotdog stand so June and I set out on our own.

We found some temporary toilets but they were unisex so we didn't hang around. Then we found a stall selling hotdogs and hamburgers and filled up. By then, I was feeling a bit more like it, a bit more ready for drinking and dancing.

'What shall we do then?' I asked June. 'Stay here or go into town?' There seemed to be plenty of people hanging around the campsite but I couldn't see anywhere where we might find music or dancing.

'Town, I reckon, don't you? We need a pub; I'm still looking for a mirror.'

We headed off in the direction of town. There were quite a few other groups of people on foot and so we followed them. As I'd thought earlier when we'd seen the scooter group in Manchester, many people looked different to our group of scooterists back home. For a start, a group ahead of us were skinheads, both girls and boys. We had skinheads down our way but they were the angry, aggressive sort that you steered clear of. Here the girls had feathered fringes around the edges of their shorn scalps and looked far less scary. They still wore the boy skinhead uniform of the Doc Martens and the too short trousers and the braces and the Ben Sherman shirts but they looked friendly enough. I could see June eyeing them up appreciatively. I wondered if it was a look that she was considering adopting herself.

I wish I'd had the chance to ask Lance what he thought June's reason for hanging out with scooterists might be. She'd never buy a scooter, she'd admitted that herself, so she wasn't really into it. June, I reckoned, was just in it for the larks. As soon as something more exciting came along, she'd be off. Or someone more exciting more like, it was probably the people she was attracted to rather than the look or the music.

One day, I thought, she would be really respectable, she'd get into management and have a manager husband and they'd have a really smart detached house that she'd keep spotlessly clean. She knew, I thought, that she had a few short years in which to be totally irresponsible and she was going to make the most of them while she could.

I needed alcohol to get loud and uninhibited, but June didn't. She was practically dancing along the front. The town seemed quite friendly for an out-of-season seaside resort. The lights had come on and the glow from the pubs along the front looked welcoming.

We chose one that had a reasonable number of scooters outside it. It also had Marvin Gaye blaring out from the juke box which seemed like a good sign. We bought a pint of snakebite each and managed to find a table over in the corner.

So far, we didn't seem to have attracted much attention. Perhaps Lance was wrong about us standing out. I managed to do a bit of people watching. There were very few girls in this pub. The lads were mostly young, teens or early twenties, and surprisingly quite a few of them had moustaches. I didn't know anyone who wore a moustache back home. For some reason it made them look as if they belonged to the army, although I didn't know whether the army allowed facial hair.

It wasn't long before we were joined at our table as a couple of lads whom June had been eyeing up at the bar came over.

'Are these seats taken?' one of them asked politely.

'Only by you,' replied June.

They introduced themselves as John and Joe from Derby. 'Members of the Lost Souls Scooter Club,' they told us proudly.

'Yeah? Where's the rest of them then?' asked June.

'Lost. Of course,' replied John.

'Yeah, he broke down just outside Derby and had to get the bus back home,' added Joe.

'So there's three of you then?' June asked.

'So far. We've only been going since March,' replied John. 'You two can join if you like. You have to attend meetings though, the first Tuesday of every month at the Golden Fleece. Derby'

'And pay subs,' added Joe.

'Do we get a badge?' I asked, 'or a patch?'

'Neither yet. But I can give you a bit of material and a felt tip pen and you can draw your own if you like,' Joe said.

'Thanks.'

I was only sipping my snakebite but it seemed to be working. I was feeling much more confident and chatty than usual.

'So are there only three scooterists in Derby?' I asked.

'Nah, there's loads,' answered Joe.

'But we fell out with most of them,' added John. 'Look, here's where the patch of our previous club used to be.' He pointed to a square gap in the middle of the patches that otherwise covered the back of Joe's jacket. Thread ends still hung from the jacket where the patch had been cut out.

'Who sews them on?' I asked.

'I got my mum to do it,' said Joe.

I quite liked the idea of someone's mum sewing on scooter patches for their son. There was something very sweet about it. I wondered if I could find a lad who sewed his patches on himself though, that really would be something.

'So how did you two get here, then?' asked John, 'because, and correct me if I'm wrong, but I don't think you're from around these parts.'

'No,' answered June, 'we got a lift with a SeaDog.'

'On a scooter?'

'No, in a car.'

'That's not allowed!'

'I know. But if we didn't come by car we wouldn't have come at all and you'd have had to have done without our company,' June retorted.

'Fair dos.'

'I have got a scooter though, but a six hundred mile round trip on it seemed a bit much,' I piped up. The lads looked interested.

'Yeah? What've you got?'

'A Vespa 100.'

'D'you get on with it?'

'I do.'

'Good. We've both got PXs.'

'Passed your test?'

'Not yet.'

'Damn it,' said June, 'I was hoping for a cruise along the front.'

'Ah well,' said Joe, 'play your cards right and you might get lucky yet.'

John and Joe were good company. I decided that I liked John best although I thought that June probably did too.

We decided to see if we could get into the all-nighter which the boys said was on further along the front. We headed out into a blast of sea air which instantly cleared my head and lifted my mood further. I felt happy and excited.

There was a queue outside the all-nighter venue even though it was early. We joined the end and edged forwards slowly. In front of us were three lads from Scotland and behind us were a gang from North Wales. Everyone was in high spirits and everyone seemed to assume that they would find common ground with complete strangers simply because they liked scooters.

'Who've we got?' Joe asked. The Scots lads named several bands. I hadn't heard of any of them but it hardly mattered. They were bound to play something we could dance to, that was the point of all-nighters.

There was a band playing Jam covers when we finally got into the hall. Joe went and got us a round of drinks. John took the opportunity to get in a bit closer to June. Oh well, I didn't mind really. I wasn't going to get off with anyone even if they asked nicely because that was what Lance was expecting me to do and I had to prove him wrong.

We hung around on the edge of the dance floor for a bit. The Mod boys were doing their stuff to 'Down in a Tube Station' but no one else was dancing much. Not surprising since it was a long time until dawn when the all-nighter would finish. The hall started to fill up. I hoped they would leave us room to breathe.

Someone pinched my bottom. I turned around quickly but couldn't see who had done it. The Jam tribute band was replaced by a band with a brass section playing fast paced soul numbers. 'Floor stompers', they were called. More people moved on to the dance floor. Most seemed to be in groups, facing each other in rough circles like girls dancing round their handbags. There was a lot of argy-bargy and you had to stand your ground in order not to get pushed over. It was good tempered though. June and I pushed our way through to a spot in the middle towards the stage. John and Joe didn't follow us. We danced for a few numbers before the band stopped for a bit of a breather.

'The sax player's a bit of alright, isn't he?' June said in my ear. I hadn't noticed so I got her to point him out to me.

'Shall we move closer to the front?' she asked, already beginning to weave her way through the crowd. I didn't really want to be up close to the speakers but I followed her anyway. As the music started up again she began to dancing for show, with an audience in mind. This required someone to dance with, so she dragged me in as a partner in her game. I was in such a good mood I joined in. To begin with we only had a tiny bit of dance floor but as we got more adventurous we grabbed a bit more space. We were getting a bit of attention and for a nasty moment it looked as though we were going to gain a circle around us so I ducked into it and forced someone else into the middle. This gave me the opportunity to look up onto the stage to see if the sax player had spotted June. I couldn't tell if he had, because he seemed to be looking at me. He saw me looking, and winked. I smiled back. I carried on dancing but more self consciously this time knowing that his eyes were on me.

I lost June in the sea of people. When the band finished their set, I fought my way back to where we had left John and Joe and our drinks. Not surprisingly they had all disappeared. I thought I'd wait for a while to see if June resurfaced. I scanned the crowd to see if I could see her. I thought briefly and rather guiltily of Ben. We'd half arranged to meet him by the hot dog stand at the campsite. We hadn't seen him there and I hadn't thought about him since. There was no point in worrying about him, he'd sort himself out somehow I thought. Probably he was here in the hall somewhere.

I caught the eye of a few lads as I looked around. I smiled generally but not anyone in particular. I wasn't going to meet anyone in here anyway as the noise level was too high and it would be as much as I could do to find out someone's name.

I decided to go and get some more drinks. It was four or five deep at the bar and I had to wait for ages to even work my way to the front. The bar staff were all girls and so although I stood there with my five pound note held out clearly they passed me by every time. Eventually in frustration I asked the bloke next to me who had just reached the front if he would add my order on to his.

Finally, having secured the drinks, I made my way carefully back to our original spot at the edge of the dance floor. June was still nowhere to be seen. I held on to both pints as I was afraid that I would lose them otherwise. This got me plenty of comments. I seemed far more attractive with two pints in front of me.

A DJ had taken over from the band. I continued to scan the dancers out on the floor. Through a brief gap between dancers I thought I saw Dave dancing face to face with Sam. I'd only actually seen them together that one time when I was waitressing so it was easy to forget that they were an item. From my brief look it was impossible to say if they were dancing up to each other or having an argument although it was probably only my wishful thinking that suggested that they might have been at odds with each other.

Just as my arm was getting tired from holding her pint, June showed up.

'Sorry,' she said, taking the glass from me, 'were you looking for me?'

'Well I did want to know where you were.' I had to shout in her ear due to the level of the music.

'I was back stage.'

I raised my eyebrows.

'Not with the saxophonist, with the singer.'

I wondered how she had managed that. Got up onstage and followed them off probably.

She looked a bit glazed and had drunk almost half her pint in one go.

'Did you have a drink back there?'

She nodded. 'They had some vodka.'

'So why did you come back?'

'They were going, got to get back to Cannock tonight, or something.'

'Anyway,' she added after a moment, 'I had to make sure you were okay didn't I?'

I gave her a quick hug across the shoulders. 'Thanks.'

The night seemed to speed up after that. I wanted to dance some more but also I didn't want to lose my pint again. I drained it as quickly as I could and joined June back on the dance floor again. There was a sense of anticipation in the air as there was a well-known soul singer due on the stage. I hadn't heard of him before but he seemed to be everything everyone was waiting for and the floor was jam-packed, with everyone concentrating on their own moves. When we emerged at the end of the set we were sweaty and exhausted.

'What time is it?' asked June.

I looked at my watch and was surprised to see it was past 2am.

'Do you want to stay here or head back to the campsite?' she asked.

'Head back,' I answered. I didn't think I could really make it through until dawn. I had heard that those who were still dancing at dawn used speed to keep them going. No one had ever offered any to me and I didn't think I would have taken it if they had. Just the name of it sounded scary.

The walk back along the front was a relief after all the noise and crush in the hall. The tide seemed to be out and there wasn't much sound coming from the sea, but still I knew it was there, I could smell it on the wind.

The walk back seemed to take no time at all but finding our tent took ages. When we'd left it we had been at the edge of the tents but since then many more had been added beyond it. We had nothing to distinguish it and no scooter left by it to recognise. In the end we chose one that looked most like it and opened the zip slowly and quietly in case we were wrong. I spotted my sleeping bag though so we crawled in and made ourselves as comfortable as we could.

'No Ben,' said June as she settled down. I grunted in return and that was the last thing we knew until mid-morning the following day.

Chapter Eight

I awoke to the sounds of scooters weaving their way past the tent. The sun was clearly high in the sky as it was heating one wall and warming my face. I felt hot and uncomfortable having spent the night fully clothed. June lay on her back, eyes open, cocooned in her sleeping bag.

'Still no Ben,' she said.

'No. Are you worried about him?'

'A bit, I suppose.'

'Did you see John or Joe again last night?' I asked.

'No. Did you?'

'No,' I answered. 'We seem to be losing people all over the place. What about your singer?'

'Well, I got his phone number,' she said, reaching into her jacket which was serving as a pillow and extracting a cigarette packet. She squinted at it. 'Alan, his name was. Give me a ring if you're ever in the Midlands, he said.'

'Not likely is it?'

'No.'

We lay there for a bit with our own thoughts.

'Well, what are we going to do?' I asked. 'I'm busting for a wee and I need a cup of tea.'

'And me. How do you get changed in a tent this size though?'

87

We wriggled about a bit, struggling with underwear and jeans, both emerging with clean tops, pants and socks but jeans, bras and jumpers remaining the same. We headed for the loos where I washed my face and hands in cold water. Then we walked over to a food stall and bought bacon sandwiches and big polystyrene cups of tea into which we tipped several sachets of sugar.

'You don't suppose Ben's still waiting by the hot dog stall do you?' asked June.

'No. Don't worry about him, he'll be okay.'

'We could put out an alert for him. 'Lost: a small curly-haired boy'.'

'Hmm. Do you think he'd answer to that description?'

'Probably not.'

We decided to see what else the campsite had to offer. There was a roped off area in the middle where there were some events scheduled. Apparently you could enter your scooter in a class and hope to win a rosette or something.

'What've they got?' asked June. 'Scooter that looks most like its owner? Waggiest aerial?'

It didn't seem as though it was the kind of thing that would attract scooterists in large numbers but if I'd found out one thing this weekend it was that there was no such thing as a typical scooterist. There were even some old blokes. Perhaps they had been Mods in the sixties and had never given their scooters up.

We went to have a look at the stalls that were lined up on the far side of the arena. Most of them carried scooter spares and accessories. I had bought a back rest and a luggage rack for mine, but still hadn't decided how or even whether to decorate it in some way. I bought a 'Morecambe 1984' patch so I could prove that I'd attended the rally.

We didn't really know what to do after that. There were plenty of people milling about on foot and on scooters but there didn't seem to be any consensus over where people were heading. We decided to walk back into town again and see what was happening there.

Again there were others heading the same way as us. The mood seemed to be more subdued than the day before. June looked a bit rough I thought. She wasn't an overly vain person but she did like to wear quite a bit of make-up. We hadn't yet found a mirror and so all she had on was the smudges of eyeliner and mascara left over from the day before. Still I didn't suppose that I looked much better.

'I need a shower,' I told her.

'Me too,' she agreed. 'Or maybe a swim.'

We both looked out to the distant sea, separated from us by a wide expanse of wet sand.

'Yeah, well, maybe not,' I said.

It was Easter Sunday so most of the shops were shut and the town had a bit of a dead air about it, despite the number of scooters and scooterists roaming the streets. There were plenty of tourists too. Elderly couples in sensible macs eyed us warily. Families kept their children close, although many of the kids looked fascinated by the scooters. They reminded me of the trip to Brighton I'd taken with my family. I began looking out for kids in their early teens embarrassed to be with their parents. I wondered if my mum would still have an Easter egg waiting for me when I got home.

A few of the kids had ice creams and we went in search of the van. June and I both bought the biggest 99s they sold and settled ourselves on a vacant stretch of sea wall. The sun was reaching over the sea now. The seagulls were squawking and circling and there was the smell of vinegar and salt mixed with the smell of the two-stroke burning off the scooters. I licked my ice cream slowly, making it last. At that moment, life felt good.

The car parked on the road in front of us left and it wasn't long before its place was taken by a group of scooterists. There were five scooters and seven lads.

One of them nodded to us. 'Alright?' he said in greeting.

'Alright,' we said in return.

'Are you local?' one of them asked us.

'No, we're from Essex.' June replied.

'Really? I've never met anyone from Essex before. Hey,' he called to his mates, 'we've got real life Essex girls here.'

Several of them looked up in interest.

'You can't tell us any joke we haven't heard already,' June said.

'What not even the fridge one?'

'Heard it.'

'What about the one about . .'

'Heard it.'

'Where's your white stilettos then?'

'At home, with the leopard skin handbag. I didn't think you lot would be sophisticated enough to appreciate it.'

'I dunno, call yourself an Essex girl. You're letting the whole side down using words like that.'

Insults over for the moment, the lads introduced themselves. They were from near Blackburn they said. Part of the Accrington Scooter Club.

'That's not a very imaginative name,' said June.

'Well we're not very imaginative people.'

'Yeah and if we've got it written down we know where we have to get back to once the rally's over.'

'Assuming you can read the word Accrington of course.'

'Yeah and find it on a map.'

One of them, Bill sat down on the wall next to me. 'Got a bit of that ice cream for me?'

'No. Get your own.'

'Charming. What's your name then?'

'Annie.'

'Nice name.'

'Thanks. I'll remember to pass that on to my mum. She gave it to me.'

Bill was a couple of years older than me I guessed. He had very straight mousy hair in a sort of overgrown Beatle moptop. Like all the lads he had army boots, jeans and a flight jacket on. He had an impressive selection of patches dating all the way back to 1982.

'I was all set up to join the army,' he told me, 'but then we went to the Falklands and I found I didn't really agree with the idea of actually fighting people so I became a scooterist instead.'

'That's not a job though.'

'No. Sadly not. Not yet anyway, but I'm working on it.'

'What do you do?'

'I'm a mechanic. Well a mechanic's assistant anyway. I hand him his oily rag.' He showed me his hands which were blackened with oil. 'How about you?'

'I'm doing catering at college.'

'Yeah? What are you going to do with that?'

'I don't know yet. A cook or a hotel manager or something in between. Maybe I'll go abroad.' I don't know why I was telling him that, it was usually something I kept to myself since people thought I was getting above myself if I revealed plans to try my luck on a cruise ship or something. Bill had the kind of manner that made me drop my guard though.

'Yeah, you should do that. Go somewhere sunny. Aim high, the Caribbean or something.

'Yeah, I might do that. I'll send a postcard shall I?'

'Or an invite to visit.'

Bill showed me his scooter. It was the standard Vespa PX125E but coated in a paint that changed from blue to green depending on how you looked at it, a bit like a two-tone suit that the ska boys wore.

'Very nice,' I said.

'Thanks. I've put a different carb and exhaust on it too, do you want me to show you those?'

'Well you can show me but don't be offended if my eyes start to glaze over at some point.'

He began to explain the finer points of his modifications. I nodded at what seemed like suitable intervals and had a look to see what June was up to. She was still on the sea wall. She had a boy on either side of her and two stood in front. She was laughing at something someone had said.

I saw her look along the front and raised her arm and call out 'Lance! Hey, Lance!'

I looked in the direction that she was looking and saw Lance approaching on foot with Perry, a couple of the other SeaDogs and some other lads I didn't recognise.

Lance saw her and nodded. He then looked around until he saw me and scowled somewhat when he saw me leaning against a scooter. He probably thought I was going to knock it over.

'You alright, girls?' he asked.

'Yes,' replied June, 'we're fine. Great in fact. You haven't seen Ben though, have you? We haven't seen him since you left us yesterday practically.'

'Ben?' He almost seemed to be wracking his brains to remember who Ben was. 'You know, I think I did see him at the all-nighter last night. Didn't speak to him though.'

Oh well at least he had been spotted. Perhaps he had stayed up all night after all. Maybe he was kipping in my tent as we spoke.

Lance was clearly not planning on sticking around and Perry and the others had already moved on further down the front.

'If you see him,' June called to his departing back, 'tell him we're looking for him.'

Lance grunted in reply without turning round.

'Did you get into the all-nighter?' Bill asked.

'Yes. Didn't you?'

'No, we didn't go until the pubs chucked out and by then it was full. They wouldn't even let us queue in case some people left early.'

'What did you do?'

'We had some beers back at the campsite. Made our own entertainment, you know?'

'And what are you doing for the rest of today?'

'We're joining the ride-out later.

'What's that?'

'Someone organises a route out of town and everyone who wants to, joins in. It's great, about the best part of the weekend, we take up the whole road and all you can see stretching ahead is scooters. Sometimes we get police escorts there's so many of us.'

'Sounds like fun,' I said.

'Yeah, it is. Then later, we'll be back at the pub again I think. The Bay, down the far end, if you're interested.'

I was interested, Bill was good company. I would have to see what June wanted though. We wandered back over to the group that was still surrounding her. A couple of the lads were clearly interested in her but the others looked a bit bored and were making noises about getting back for the ride out.

Someone said 'hello', loudly behind me. I turned to see it was John from the night before.

'What happened to you?' June shouted over my head.

'We were just about to ask you the same thing,' replied John. He looked a bit pissed off, perhaps at the sight of the Accrington lads. I thought about introducing them and then decided against it. There didn't seem to be too much each of us wanted to say to the other and so they nodded and wandered off again.

'See you in Torquay perhaps,' said Joe as they left.

I did think that Lance had been proved wrong so far. Everyone we met had been as polite as you could wish for and no one had tried anything on at all. Lance definitely had a poor impression of his fellow scooterists. There had been a few rude remarks but nothing more than you might expect walking down the high street at home.

After the Accrington boys left, June and I were on our own again. We spent the afternoon quite happily enough exploring the front and the town. As the evening drew on we decided to head to a pub for a drink or three. We found the pub that

Bill had mentioned earlier and as it looked quite a cheery place, we went in.

We'd managed two pints each before any of the Accrington boys came in. Bill wasn't among them and while the others nodded and said hello, they didn't join us. We continued to drink steadily and June moved on to vodka. The pubs were supposed to close at 10.30, it being a Sunday. We got a lock-in for a while but eventually got turfed out on to the streets.

I was feeling a bit thick headed from the drink and wanted to sit down for a while. We found a wall near the entrance to the pier where a group of scooterists had gathered. It seemed there had been some sort of a fight between locals and scooterists and everyone was hanging around to see if it would kick off again. I was happy enough sitting there and listening in on conversations.

Someone put a hand on my shoulder. I jumped and looked up. It was John, or was it Joe? No, John, the taller one. Joe was over by June who was on the edge of the crowd but slowly getting swallowed up by it.

'Hi,' he said.

'Hi,' I replied.

'Good evening?' he asked.

'Okay. The all-nighter was better.'

'Yeah, you meet anyone tonight? You seem to have blokes swarming over you.' He seemed a bit drunk and a bit angry.

'Hardly.'

The crowd was moving about. I spotted the police on the far side moving people along. It seemed that the show was over. I looked for June again but she was nowhere in sight. I stood on the wall in order to see better but I still could not spot her in the crowd. I climbed down. I seemed to be making a habit of losing people.

John was still there though.

'I've lost June,' I told him.

'Then I've lost Joe. They'll be okay together,' he said. 'We could walk back to the campsite if you like.'

I figured that's what June would do. 'Okay.'

We set off back down the front. John didn't say much. All of a sudden he grabbed my hand. 'Come on down here,' he said pulling me down some steps that led on to the beach. I had no choice but to follow him.

I did feel attracted to him but he moved too fast and too forcefully. Before I knew it he had my back up against the sea wall. He forced his knee between my legs and began grinding his lips on to mine. I was instantly repulsed and used all my might to force him off.

'Get off,' I shouted.

'Don't be so mardy. You know you want it. You were giving me the eye yesterday,' he said angrily.

'That doesn't mean I want a quick one against a wall,' I said, wiping my mouth. It seemed as though he had drawn blood.

'Well maybe you won't get a say in it.' He was back on me again. My head hit the stones behind me and I was temporarily disorientated. He got his hands under my jumper and began groping at my breasts.

'Not got much, have you?'

'I said, get off!' I repeated, beginning to cry. There was a shout from above me somewhere.

'Oi, you. Leave her alone,' said the voice.

John moved away from me.

'Frigid bitch.' He spat at me, catching me in the face.

I sank to my knees, my face in my hands as he strode off up the beach. Someone crouched down in front of me and pulled my hands gently away from my face.

'Are you okay?' I recognised the voice and looked up. It was Lance.

I nodded. 'I wasn't .. I didn't . . .'

'I know.'

He pulled me to my feet. I was shaking and he grasped both of my hands to steady me.

'Where's June?'

'I don't know. I lost her by the pier.'

'Is she okay, do you think?'

I shrugged. 'I don't know.'

'Look let's get back up on the front,' he said.

Lance helped me back up the steps I had been pulled down earlier and sat me down on the sea wall.

'Who was he?'

'A lad from Derby. We met them in the pub yesterday. He was a bit drunk, I think.'

I was still shaking. Lance looked tired.

'See,' he said softly. I thought he was thinking about how he'd had to become responsible for me, even though he said he wouldn't.

'Look, I can't drive you back to the campsite because I've had a few drinks. I can't let you stay in my room because I'm sharing with Perry. I could put you in a taxi but then I'd be worried about whether you had reached the other end safely.'

'Don't worry about me,' I said. 'I can walk back, he didn't hurt me and I don't suppose I'll meet him again.'

'You can't say that for sure. Where's June? You two should've stuck together.'

'I know,' I said miserably.

'You could sleep in the car if you wanted. I'll bring some blankets down and you can lock yourself in.' Suddenly I felt so tired; I just wanted to be curled up, under covers, somewhere safe. But there wasn't anywhere safe here, I was too far away from home. I wasn't sure whether the car was the best bet but I didn't fancy walking all the way back to the campsite on my own.

I nodded, 'Okay.'

'Come on then.'

We crossed the road and headed back into town away from the front. I stuffed my hands into my pockets and hunched my shoulders. Lance looked at me. He held out his hand. I wasn't sure what he wanted. I looked at his hand and then looked at him and then finally, unearthed my own hand from my pocket and slid it into his. Although it was the second time that I had held hands with

99

someone in the space of an hour, this felt odd. Lance didn't strike me as a person who would hold anybody's hand. But it was warm and well-meant and I settled into it as much as I was able. I wondered what June's response would be if she saw us walking down the street like this.

Neither of us spoke until we reached the car. Lance let my hand go and I stuffed it back in my pocket in order to preserve the warmth that we had created. He opened the car.

'Right,' he said, 'the passenger seat goes all the way back till it's nearly flat.' He demonstrated this. Or you could use the back seat but you won't be able to lie flat there.' It sounded as if he had slept in the car on more than a few occasions.

'I'll try the front then.'

I got in.

'I'll go and see if I can borrow some blankets then,' said Lance and he disappeared into the Bed and Breakfast, reappearing a few minutes later with two blankets and a pillow.

'The landlady doesn't know I've got these so we'll have to sneak them back in in the morning.'

'Here's a spare key,' he continued, 'and you can lock all the doors by locking the driver's side.'

'Okay,' I said. 'And . . .thanks.'

'That's alright. I hope you'll be okay.'

He left me to it. I had never slept in a car before and I felt a bit exposed. There were quite a few people still about the streets. I curled up so as much of me was under the blankets as possible and tried to make myself look like a pile of clothing.

No one bothered me though and eventually I drifted off to sleep.

Chapter Nine

I awoke to the sound of someone tapping on glass. I blinked a few times trying to get my surroundings into focus. I realised I was in the car and recalled what had happened the previous evening. It was Lance knocking on the window. I sat up and unlocked the doors. He came round and sat himself in the driver's seat.

'Are you okay? Did you sleep?'

'Yes, a bit.'

'Good. I thought perhaps Perry and I should have had the car and let you have our room.

'No. That would have been too much. I was alright.' I looked at my watch, it was 7am.

'I know it's early,' he said, 'but I'm usually up before 6, so this is late for me.' He seemed really chatty this morning. Perhaps we had broken the ice with whatever happened the night before.

'Look, I'm worried about June. We don't know that she got back to the campsite. I thought we should go and look.'

'Yes, you're right. I still don't know where Ben is either.'

'Ah. Now Ben I do know about. He's making his own way back.'

'Why?'

'I'll leave that up to Ben to tell you. All you need to know is that he is in one piece, although he's quite lucky because he nearly wasn't.'

'Oh.'

I unravelled myself from the blankets and folded them up as best I could as Lance started up the engine.

The campsite looked like a three day party had just ended. Every space between tents and scooters was littered with cans and bottles and food wrappers and flyers. I was embarrassed to see it. Surely we could be a bit more responsible than that, I thought.

A few scooterists were up and about. Some were making preparations to leave. I led Lance across the site towards our tent. From the outside I couldn't tell if anyone was inside so I knelt down and undid the zip quietly.

There was a mound inside, quite a large mound. I wondered if I'd got the wrong tent.

'June?' I said tentatively. Something moved and I saw June's bleached head lift up.

'Whass up?' she said groggily.

'It's okay. It's only me, Annie.' I realised that she lay entwined with a boy. I could see his DMs poking out from under my sleeping bag which he seemed to be using as a blanket. I wondered if it was Joe.

'Look, I'll come back in a bit, okay?'

'Okay. Look we'll get up now.'

'Don't worry. I'll see you in an hour or so. Don't go from here.'

I did the zip up again and stood up.

'It's alright,' I said to Lance,' it's her in there.'

'Oh good.' He seemed relieved.

'Will you go back to your digs now?' I asked.

'In a bit. I'll get some breakfast here first I think. Do you want something?'

I nodded and we headed off to the nearest food stall. After three days of fried food I could have done with some cereal or fruit or something but since the choice was bacon sandwich or bacon roll, I had a sandwich.

Lance and I sat down on some plastic chairs by the stall and ate our breakfast. Parts of me were sore from a night trying to fit the shape of the car seat. I twisted and stretched my body around a bit in order to try and straighten myself out.

'You know,' I said to Lance, 'I've thought about what you said when you were wondering why I had bought a scooter.'

'Oh yeah? People don't usually think about what I've said.'

'I bet they do. Everyone respects you.'

'They do?'

'Yeah. Anyway, I think I have an answer, kind of.'

'Go on.'

'Well, you know what you said about those people who want to say something about themselves by riding a scooter? You called them posers. And you said that I wasn't one because I'm too quiet?'

'Yes, I remember.'

'Well I think that maybe quiet people want to say something to other people about themselves too.'

'So that's what you're trying to do?'

'I think so.'

'So what are you trying to say?'

'Well, you know, I was in Brighton with my family three Easters ago and saw all the Mods there and I liked the look of them. They were different from anyone I knew but they were all similar. It was like they were saying that they weren't going to be normal and boring and that life was about fun things that didn't have anything to do with learning or working or anything and I hadn't really come across that before, everything had some kind of underlying aim of improvement, so I would come out of it a better person, but this wasn't anything to do with that.'

'So you were attracted by its aimlessness?'

'Not really, more the . . . shift of focus, that you could just pass your time hanging out and by wearing the right clothes and stuff you'd automatically hang out with people who understood you.'

'Okay.'

'But I did that, I wore the right clothes and got the right look, but I found out that that wasn't enough because I wanted to hang out with the boys and they were suspicious of me because I was a girl. This was at school by the way.'

Lance was looking a closely at me, it seemed he was trying to understand although I didn't think I was making much sense.

'No one had a scooter at our school. Not until the fifth year and a new boy joined and he had a Vespa 50 that he used to ride in sometimes. And he was what I wanted to be. He wasn't the same, because he was new, and he wasn't the same because he could go where he wanted when he wanted and when he wanted to be on his own, he could go and hang out on his scooter and when he wanted others to be impressed by him he could go and hang out on his scooter and he could say everything he wanted people to know about him without actually having to tell them. And some people might have thought he was odd and some people might have thought he was arrogant but that's okay because he'd never have got on with those people anyway so it was like a short cut to finding friends. And it was the scooter that did it in the way that a parka wouldn't have.'

'So were you friends with him?'

'No. It turned out he was way too arrogant.'

Lance laughed.

'But the thing is, I could have been, I would have been because he was the real deal.'

'So what you're saying is, I think, you want to be part of this movement because it represents something outside of normal life and you need a scooter as entry.'

'Yes, I suppose, something like that. People like June, they don't need to fit in and so they can be on the edges quite happily. I need to be accepted. And it worked. Dave only spoke to me because I have a scooter and now I think I can call him a friend, or at least someone I know. And through knowing him and Ben, now I know you and you're about as authentic as you can get.'

'How do you mean?'

'Well you were there first, you fit, you call the shots, no one asks you why you're a scooter boy, you just are.' I thought for a moment. 'Do you think you always will be?'

'Yeah. In some form or another.'

'Anyway to get back to the boy-girl thing, I could never be a Mod could I? Mods are boys. I could be a Modette but that just means a hanger-on basically – a second-class Mod because I'm a girl. But this,' I waved my hands to encompass the whole rally, 'there's scooter boys and there's scooter girls and I can be a scooter girl if I want, but I can also be a scooterist and then it doesn't matter if I'm a boy or a girl. If I've got a scooter then I am one.'

'But it's still run by blokes, it's a blokes' idea. Do you think we'd have all this,' he mimicked my rally-encompassing gesture, 'if it was organised by girls?'

'Well . . .'

'No. We'd have half a dozen of us riding carefully to a tea room about twenty minutes from home, a couple of scones, a nice cup of tea and then back in time for your favourite television programme.'

'That's a bit unkind, we're not all old biddies, you know.'

'I know that. What I'm trying to say, in my cack-handed way, is that, left to you you'd never have come up with the idea. If women ruled the world we wouldn't have scooters or even cars because you wouldn't have thought them necessary. We wouldn't even have had the industrial revolution because inventing stuff isn't what drives you.'

I opened my mouth to speak.

'And that isn't a criticism,' he added before I could say anything. 'I'm not saying you're wrong to want to be part of this. But you can't go into it expecting to be treated the same as blokes. We're different, you and I, and if we ignore that we're not doing each other any favours. Look at the old Mods from the sixties, some of them have still got their scooters. In twenty years' time, I'll probably still have mine, I'll probably have a garage of them and that'll be okay for me. But you will have moved on, you'll have different concerns. Occasionally you'll remember that you had a scooter once but you won't want to own one again.'

'So why will it be okay for you?'

'Cos I'm a bloke and blokes never grow up do they? What we're doing here is just a bigger version of playing with toys. We're all trying to prove we've got the biggest, best and shiniest tractor, that's all. Do you know I drive a forklift for a living?'

I did, of course, but I shook my head. Lance changed tack.

'You know,' he said, 'maybe it's a freedom thing. Boys have always had more freedom than girls. So we can do this sort of thing and no one's going to question whether we should be allowed to. But I bet it's different with you. What did your parents say when you said you were coming here?'

'Well they weren't too keen.'

'You see, you're railing against all these . . ' he sought for the right word, 'constraints, all these constraints put upon girls that just don't exist for boys.'

'Perhaps.'

'But, you know, it's not that great being a bloke either. Blokes are ugly and aggressive and irresponsible and always looking to score points.'

'You don't rate your sex very highly.'

'No, I don't.'

We lapsed into silence. After a while Lance stood up. 'Look, I'd better go back and see what's up with Dave, okay?'

'Okay.'

'Be in the car park at 1pm like we said.'

'Okay. Lance . . .,' I said just as he was about to leave,' thanks, you know . . .'

He nodded and disappeared off amongst the tents.

I was reluctant to return to my tent. I thought that Joe, if it was Joe, might still be there and I didn't want to see him. I didn't really want to tell June about what had happened last night either. I stayed where I was at the food stall for a while, until it became clear that I was in the way, as the bacon roll rush began.

I headed back to the tent via the loos. Many of the tents had been taken down and I could see June sat outside ours as I picked my way through the rubbish on the ground. She looked up as she saw me coming. I sat down next to her.

'Can we talk about it later?' I asked. She nodded.

109

'Are you okay though?' she asked.

'Yes. I slept in the car, Lance's car.'

'At least you were safe, I didn't know.'

'No, me either.'

'Shall we take the tent down then?'

'Yes, there's no one in it is there?'

'No, he's gone.'

Taking the tent down was easier than putting it up although getting it back into the bag again was a challenge. June and I were both a bit nervous of each other. There seemed to be a feeling that we'd let each other down somehow. She said that she and Joe had looked for me but had eventually decided that I must be back at the tent and that when I was wasn't there, she'd asked Joe to stay.

I told her about what had happened to me and she wanted to find John and have a go at him but I didn't want anything more to do with him. I painted Lance as my knight in shining armour. June seemed appalled that he had made me sleep in the car while he'd slept in his bed, but I thought it was the right solution.

I thought perhaps I'd fallen a little in love with Lance, so that anything he did was okay by me. I wanted to have some time to think about some of the things he'd said, to think about how he'd held my hand on the way back to the car. I decided to store it all away somewhere to think about later when I had some space to do so.

We made it back to the car park at the correct time and Lance and Dave showed up as they said they would. Dave was very subdued but would not reveal why. I said that I thought I had seen him

110

at the all-nighter and he agreed that he had been there but wouldn't give any more details about his weekend. June met with a similar block when she tried to find out about what had happened to Ben.

As we drove out of Morecambe we lapsed into silence. Lance put some music on and we all listened to it but no one sang. I wondered if he would stop at the beauty spot we had stopped at on the way up but we didn't even seem to go past it.

It was early evening by the time we were almost home. I still had to get back from town. I was assuming that Lance would drop us off at the Red Cow, but he drove through streets of houses before pulling up outside one. It turned out to be Dave's. He got out and mumbled his goodbyes.

Lance turned round to us.

'I'll drive you girls home if you like,' he said to us.

'I live out of town,' I warned him.

'I know, and that's okay.'

He dropped June off first. She said goodbye and we arranged to meet for a day before we were back at college.

'Come and sit in the front,' Lance said, 'I don't want to feel like I'm driving a taxi.'

I had only been away three days and yet it felt as though I was returning to a different country. I looked at the familiar landscape through new eyes. I was pleased to be back, I wanted to sleep in my own bed and to know that my Mum was near if I needed her.

As we pulled up in our cul-de-sac, I asked Lance if he wanted to come in for a cup of tea. To my surprise, he said yes. I was pleased. I thought it might be good for my parents to meet him, perhaps they might trust me a little more if I went on other trips in the future. They were delighted to see me return in one piece and intrigued to see me bring a boy back. Mum was all over him, offering him biscuits, toast, a cooked dinner. He answered all their questions carefully but soon made his escape. I couldn't blame him. I walked back out to the car with him.

'I keep feeling the need to say thank you,' I said.

'Yeah, well don't. I do what I do because I want to, not because I'm looking for gratitude,' he replied. He had his hand on the door handle but then changed his mind and moved towards me. Quickly he dropped a kiss on the end of my nose. I just looked at him.

'I'll see you,' he said although he didn't say when or where. He got in the car and drove off. I watched him leave.

As I walked back into the house, Mum said 'He seems nice, Annie. Is he your boyfriend?' Perhaps, I thought, it hadn't been such a good idea to invite him in after all.

Chapter Ten

I slept through most of Tuesday and moped around most of Wednesday. On Thursday I watched television. I couldn't think what to do with myself. I went for a couple of rides on my scooter but couldn't really think of anywhere to go. I was waiting for something, but I wasn't sure what. Lance wasn't going to ring as he didn't have my number. I half hoped he would show up at the house now he knew where I lived and kept an ear out for any scooter sounds, but of course I didn't hear any.

On Friday, I rode up to June's house. She was bursting with gossip, having seen Ben and got his story out of him.

'You'll never guess,' she began when we were settled in her bedroom with tea and toast, 'he only got off with Sam.'

'Dave's Sam?'

'Yes, well not Dave's Sam anymore. Which means he's back on the market,' she added.

'How did that happen then?'

'Well Ben was a bit cagey about it as you can imagine, but what I think happened was that Dave and Sam had some sort of argument at the all-nighter on the Saturday night. Ben bumped into Sam after that and she ended up taking him back to the room at the B&B and locking Dave out. He stayed at the all-nighter and so didn't realise till he got back in the morning.'

'Blimey,' I said, as it seemed the only suitable response.

'Yes, I know. Apparently Sam came straight out and told Dave that she'd got off with Ben. He'd have been quite happy to have kept it quiet he said.'

'Blimey,' I said again. 'So what happened after that?'

'Well you know Dave, he's not really the sort to have a fight is he?' So he just walked away. He told Sam he didn't care. '

'I bet he does. You saw him on the way home.'

'Yeah, anyway Lance and Perry got involved and they all told Ben to make his own way home. He said it took him forever 'cos it was a bank holiday.'

'Well, it serves him right. What made him shag Sam anyway?'

'I expect he thought it was his only opportunity.'

'Even so.'

'Yeah. He said he wished he hadn't. He keeps calling Sam but she won't answer and of course his name is mud with the SeaDogs.'

'So we won't be seeing him up at the Red Cow for a bit.'

'Probably not.'

'What about Sam? She can't be very popular either.'

'I don't know about her. I haven't heard that side of the story.'

'I bet you're dying to though.'

'You bet. Shall we go up the Red Cow next week?'

I agreed to go, although not for the same reason as June.

We were back at college on the following Monday. It was nearly May, which meant there was another bank holiday and another scooter rally in a week or so. This one was to Torquay which was nearly as far as Morecambe only heading south-west rather than north. I knew I wouldn't be going to that one. I hoped for Lance's sake that he would have his scooter back on the road in time so he could have a proper rally without the hassle of all of us hangers on.

His comments at Morecambe had got me wondering about who I thought I was and who I wanted to be. I'd only really signed up for the catering course because I wanted to leave school and because I'd once been impressed with a friend's brother's ability to cut up a whole cucumber in a few seconds. I didn't know what job I wanted to do at the end of it at all. I had thought of finding work abroad, as I'd confessed to Bill, but I didn't know where I could go or what sort of a job I could do.

I was getting on well with my scooter now. It was beginning to be less a statement of image and more a daily pleasure, like some people do the crossword or drink coffee. I enjoyed the whole ritual of getting ready to ride and I enjoyed the little thrill every time I accelerated away from the kerb, knowing I was in control. It seemed to be another friend and I looked forward to walking out into the car park and seeing it there. I had never got used thinking of it as a him. June referred to Luigi occasionally I always had to wrack my brains for who or what she was talking about.

Riding up to the Red Cow on Wednesday evening, I wasn't thinking about who would be there, I was just enjoying the journey. I was disappointed to find though that there was no one I knew in the car park. I parked up anyway. There were only about a dozen scooters there. It looked as though it was going to be a quiet night.

June showed up and we went inside to dance. There was no one that we knew in there either. Some of the Sessex Girls were there, but not Sam and some of the SeaDogs but not Lance or Dave. We stayed until it was time for June's last bus anyway, making the most of emptier dance floor to practise our steps.

I walked over to my scooter alone. I was surprised to see someone sitting on it. It was Dave. I wondered how he'd got there; he still had his cast on so he couldn't have come by scooter.

'Hello,' I said.

'Hi, I was hoping to see you. I expect you've heard by now. About Sam and me that is.'

'Yes. June saw Ben. I think he's very sorry, if that helps.' I wasn't sure that he was actually, but I felt someone should try and smooth things over.

'Yeah, well, I expect I'll forgive him in time. Sam was probably more to blame than him. Is she in there?'

'No, Suzy and Karen are, but not Sam, or Ben. Or Lance.'

'No, he's been spending all his spare hours trying to get his scoot on the road.'

'Is he going to do it? In time for Torquay I mean?'

'Don't know yet. So far, it's looking good, but he's only got two more days left.'

'Why did you want to see me anyway?'

'Oh, well I wondered, since most of my mates will be away at the weekend, whether you wanted to do something.'

It was a funny way of asking but I wasn't going to pass up the chance to spend time with Dave just because he was only asking me because everyone else was busy.

'Yes. That would be nice. Do you have anything in mind?'

'Well, West Ham are playing at home on Saturday. Against Aston Villa. We could go and see the match if you wanted.'

I was a bit confused, a football match was a funny first date. Still, no boy had asked me to go anywhere before so I wasn't going to be picky. It did make me think that this wasn't supposed to be a proper date though.

'I've never been to a football match before,' I admitted

'That'll make it all the more exciting then,' he said.

We agreed a time to meet by the train station on Saturday morning and Dave wandered off into the gloom of the evening.

I couldn't quite understand why he had asked, but I was quite excited. Even the idea of going to a football match gave me a thrill. Dad was a West Ham supporter and went to matches now and again with a couple of old school friends. I had asked him to take me a number of times but he never would. He always said it wasn't the place for a girl.

Dave was waiting for me at the station when I arrived on Saturday. He'd bought the tickets and was kitted out in a claret and blue football top and a claret and blue scarf. He gave this to me. 'So everyone knows who you support,' he said.

'But I might not support West Ham.'

'Doesn't matter, Villa are claret and blue as well. Don't shout for them, though will you, it'll be all West Ham down our end.'

The train, when it came, was already pretty full but we managed to find two seats opposite a couple who seemed to be on their way to see a musical in the West End. They looked about the same age as us, but were completely different otherwise. I marvelled at their neat clothes and the fact that a boy of my age might willingly spend an afternoon in a theatre. We eyed each other warily.

'So did Lance get to Torquay?' I asked Dave.

'Well I saw him last night and he was all packed up and ready to go. There's six of them

118

going together – all the SeaDogs except for me, so he'll be okay if he does break down.'

'Your scootering season's not going too well so far is it?'

'You mean what with breaking my arm and losing my girlfriend?'

'Well I really only meant breaking your arm, but I suppose the other thing's not good either,' I said, flustered. I hadn't meant to bring the whole Sam thing up.

'No. On the plus side, I should have this cast off for Yarmouth.' He didn't say what he thought his girlfriend situation would be by then.

We had to travel in to Liverpool Street and then back out again on the District Line to get to West Ham. 'Upton Park, actually,' said Dave, 'You only make that mistake once.'

The tube train was already full of football supporters and became fuller at each stop. Dave and I were holding on to the same hand rail and got squashed closer and closer as more people piled on. It made me realise how tall he was as my head barely made it to his shoulder. I was so close to him, I could smell his sweat. It was a masculine smell, kind of sweet but peppery somehow. It smelt good.

The mood was generally good amongst the supporters. We emerged at Upton Park station and Dave thought we had time for a drink so we headed for a pub close by. This was packed so I let him squeeze his way to the bar for drinks while I found a small space and tried to hold my ground. Everyone seemed to be talking knowledgeably about the football and predicting how the match would go and how the season would end. You had to have an opinion, it seemed. I thought I'd keep my mouth shut. If I avoided asking any questions no one would know how clueless I was.

Dave appeared with a pint for him and a half for me that he was clutching unsteadily in the hand with the cast on it. We drank them and set off for the ground. Everyone it seemed was heading in the same direction. There was an air of anticipation. It reminded me of the scooter rally. Again, the crowd was mostly male.

There were houses on either side of the street we were walking down. A bit further along there was a covered market. Lettuce leaves and other food stuffs littered the floor. The shoppers were mostly Asian and seemed to be oblivious to the mainly white crowds heading towards the football ground.

I could see the ground up ahead of us now. I had imagined an imposing entrance so was quite surprised to see we had to enter down a narrow drive, past the supporters' shop which was housed in a portakabin. We joined the queue to pay at the turnstiles. There were a good number of police about but they weren't bothering anyone.

Dave seemed buoyed up by the occasion. He was bouncing on the balls of his feet, humming softly to himself. He paid for both of us and we walked through into the stands. Ahead of me were concrete tiers that climbed high up under a metal roof. They seemed to be at least half full already.

'I usually go over in the other corner,' said Dave. 'Follow me.'

We wriggled our way through past beer bellies and lit cigarettes to the far side and, having found a suitable spot, stood facing the pitch. Old pop tunes were blasting out of some ropey sounding speakers and several players were on the pitch warming up.

'That's Villa,' Dave explained.

The conversations around me were scathing about the opposition and peppered with swear words. They seemed to be the only adjectives people knew. There was an older woman a few tiers in front of me who was loudly fucking this and fucking that. She also seemed to know everyone. I was still afraid to speak, in case I revealed my ignorance and showed Dave up.

'You're very quiet,' he said eventually.

'Yes, I'm just soaking it all up,' I replied.

'I was beginning to worry. I thought you might be shocked by all the language.'

'Well I am a bit, but you soon become used to it, don't you. It's just another word,' I said.

It was getting closer to kick off and all of a sudden, crowds seemed to surge into the stands from the right. I thought I had a pretty clear view of the pitch but two tall men took the space on the tier in front of me and I had to move so as not to be looking straight into the back of one of their heads.

'We should have brought you a milk crate. My dad used to bring one for me when I was little,' Dave said.

'I'm not little.'

'No, well, short then.'

'I'm not short! I'm average.'

'For a girl, not for someone in a football crowd.'

The players appeared on the pitch to a roar of approval from the crowd. Names were read out and some received huge cheers.

The match started and West Ham were aiming for the goal in front of us. The first time they approached us the crowd surged forwards. I wasn't ready for it and lost my footing, falling onto one of the men in front of me. They weren't amused.

'Fucking stand your ground, can't you?' said one of them.

Go down the front with the other kids,' said the other, elbowing me upwards.

I righted myself, blushing both from embarrassment and from getting a faceful of donkey jacket. Dave seemed embarrassed for me. He tried putting an arm across my shoulders but that seemed unsuitably intimate in the circumstances. I shrugged him off and he seemed offended.

The next time the crowd surged forwards I was ready for it. I stood my ground and took the force on my shoulders. Something hard hit the top of my head. I rubbed my scalp and saw blood on my fingers. I wanted to shout and swear at whoever had thrown the object. Within twenty minutes of my first football match it seemed I had become aggressive in a way that was unfamiliar to me.

No one scored in the first half.

'I can't believe it, fucking nil-nil,' I said to Dave at half time. It was supposed to be a joke but he looked shocked at my language.

He wandered off to get us a burger and left me on my own on the terraces. I flicked through the programme he had bought, trying to see if I could recognise any names. There was Trevor Brooking; Dad had always gone on about him. He called him The Gentleman of Football as if there were only one.

Someone sidled up next to me, an older man.

'You on your own, love?' he asked.

'No, my friend will be back in a moment,' I replied concentrating on the programme.

'Do you fancy coming outside with me?'

'Er , no.' Why was he asking me this? I looked him in the face briefly and wished I hadn't; he had a kind of greedy look about him. I turned away. 'No thank you,' I repeated.

'Go on, just a quick one, I'll make it worth your while.'

I was horrified. No one around me seemed to have noticed what this man was doing, but why would they?

'I said no thank you.' I spoke loudly, hoping to attract some attention. He put his hand on my bottom. 'Get your hand off me. Please go away.' I said. I tried to wriggle away from him. I hoped Dave was on his way back.

'Excuse me, love, is this man bothering you?' someone said.

'Yes he is,' I replied gratefully.

A big bald man in a hooded top from about two tiers above me grabbed the jacket of my attacker and wrenched him off me.

'I heard the lady asking you to leave her alone, so do us all a favour and fuck off, okay?' the bald man shouted loudly in his ear.

'You can't blame a bloke for trying,' the older man said as he made his way through the crowd. The bald man aimed a kick at his departing back.

'Thank you,' I said.

'S'alright love. Sorry I didn't stop him earlier. Don't let him put you off the Hammers, he was probably a Spurs fan got lost.'

I managed a smile even though I felt on the verge of tears. It was at this point that Dave returned, a burger in each hand and a coke in each pocket. He saw me talking to the bald man and gave him a dirty look.

'You've got the wrong bloke,' I told him, 'he just pulled someone off me.'

'Who?'

'Some old bloke. He . . . propositioned me and felt me up.'

Dave stood there, speechless, still holding the burgers. I took one off him to help him out even though I didn't really fancy it.

'You want to look after her better,' the bald man shouted down to Dave.

'Yes. Thanks,' said Dave. He ate his burger. I picked at mine. Eventually he spoke.

'Sorry, I don't think I thought this through.'

'Don't blame yourself. It's a public place, anything might happen.' I didn't want him to get the impression that it wasn't safe for me to be out. I didn't need wrapping in cotton wool.

'Do you want to get out of here?'

'No. I want to see how the game ends,' I said. 'Perhaps we could find somewhere a bit less crowded though.'

Dave agreed. We headed back towards the exit and then up the side of the stands to the top where we were above the bulk of the crowd. Here there was enough space to sit down. The match restarted and Dave stood to see what was going on on the pitch. I stayed sat down though. I was thinking about Lance's comments about how men would try to take advantage. I had thought I was safe but twice recently I had been in situations where large groups of men were gathered together and twice I had received unwelcome attention from them. But he was wrong in saying that I would be flattered by the attention, both times I had been repulsed and left shaking and feeling violated.

What Lance hadn't understood was that neither of my attackers had any thought for or about me. They weren't coming on to me because they found me attractive. They knew or cared nothing of my personality and since in neither case was I dressed to attract attention did they know anything about my physical qualities. So the only reason that they thought they could make an advance had to be because I was female. Female and vulnerable. And I wasn't going to be flattered by attention that had no sense of me as a person.

It bothered me that both times I had to rely on someone else to scare the attacker away. I had neither the words or the strength to do it myself. While I didn't want these situations to occur in the first place, I didn't want to be dependent on another man to save me. I didn't want to feel weak. Wasn't that the feeling that having a scooter was supposed to overcome?

I supposed I should be thankful that the majority of the men I encountered were uninterested in me as a sexual object and that a few of them were prepared to step in to help me out. It showed that despite what Lance thought, blokes on the whole were generally okay.

With all these thoughts whirling round in my head, I got up and went to stand next to Dave. From the top of the stands you could only see the nearer section of the pitch since the roof came low and obscured the far goal. It didn't matter because all the action was up our end which meant that Aston Villa were getting the better of the game. Below me the crowd were shouting both encouragements and abuse at the players. One portion of the crowd seemed to take exception to the referee. They appeared to think that he was making some unfair decisions. At one point they began singing the words 'We want a referee' to the tune of 'Those were the Days my Friend' by Mary Hopkins. That cheered me up, I thought it was quite clever.

When Aston Villa scored, the West Ham fans went quiet for a moment before beginning their encouragement and abuse again. If you were going to pick a bloke as a boyfriend out of this lot, I thought, you would have to go for one who preferred the encouragement option.

Dave occasionally called out, 'Come on you Irons,' and joined in with a chorus of 'Johnny Lyall's claret and blue army,' but he wasn't as engrossed in responding to the action on the pitch in the same way as some of the others. I thought of plenty of questions I could ask him about the game but I didn't ask any of them.

I thought I could ask him why he was into football in the same way that Lance had asked me why I was into scooters. There was something about Dave that made him stand apart from most of the football crowd although I couldn't work out what it was. Perhaps it was my presence; maybe I was holding him back.

The match ended one – nil to Aston Villa and the crowd were reduced to grumbling about small points in the match where a player hadn't performed in the way that they felt he should, or where a decision had not gone West Ham's way. We all had to file out through the exit and back down the drive. Dave and I were at the end of the queue and it took us a long time to exit and reach the tube station. We couldn't even get in to the station. There were barriers up creating a queue that snaked out of the entrance and round down a side road. We joined the end of it. Policemen on horses were patrolling the line and keeping it in order. There seemed to be a lot of resentment of their presence now as if we couldn't be trusted to queue successfully on our own. I felt a certain solidarity with the queue members, it felt as if we were all in this together. Stragglers continued to come down the road to join the end of the queue. Some saw the length of it and attempted to duck under the barriers to jump in closer to the front. The police were swift to pull them out. Then I saw a white girl with a black man, clearly a couple. A voice behind me said:

'I don't mind 'em, but I don't like to see 'em with one of our girls.' My sense of solidarity was gone. I just wanted to get on the train and get home.

Dave seemed to have clammed up completely. I wished I knew him well enough to ask him what he was thinking, but I didn't think I did yet. I didn't know if he knew about the incident at Morecambe. I hoped not or it would make me seem a little accident-prone. I wondered about other girls. June, I thought, would have both the words and the strength to see an attacker off. And I knew she *would* see him off.

I wondered if any girl would have not fought. If they would have let John have his way, or, worse even, have gone outside with that man when he asked them to. I shuddered at the thought. But if the men didn't have much chance of success, why did they try it on in the first place? I used to think that I could understand people but I was beginning to think that I never would, that we didn't all grow up with the same morals and the same way of seeing things, that there wasn't respect for our fellow humans. I wondered if these self-centred traits were just a male thing or if girls could act like that too. I wondered if I could act like that if I closed my mind to certain beliefs that I held because I had been taught that this was the right way to be and to act. I didn't think I could and I was certain that I didn't want to.

When we got back to town, Dave walked me back to my scooter. It seemed to remind him of the rallies and we had something to talk about again.

'I should have my cast off in a couple of weeks,' he said.

'In time for Yarmouth,' I replied.

'Yes, I hope so. Are you going?'

'I don't know. I could ride up this time. Yarmouth's not that far is it? But I don't have anyone to ride up with.'

'Oh. I'll be going with the SeaDogs.'

This seemed to mean that he wouldn't be able to go with me, since I wouldn't be invited to go with them.

'Maybe I'll see if Ben's going.' I looked to see Dave's reaction to this, but he didn't give one. I pulled my helmet on, and kick-started the engine.

'See you then,' I said as I prepared to pull away.

'See you.' He held his hand up to say goodbye. As I moved off I looked behind me to see if it was safe to cross to the middle of the road to make a turn and caught a brief glimpse of Dave. He was still stood there with his hand up.

Chapter Eleven

I saw Ben the following Friday when he came to a disco at the college. June had invited him. He didn't want to talk much about Morecambe and I didn't press him for details. He said that he thought he would go to Yarmouth and that he was planning to ride up with a couple of Tom's friends from Southend on the Friday and that I was welcome to join them if I wanted.

The disco was fun. I liked most of the others on my course and quite a few of them had shown up. We found a couple of tables together and settled in for a good evening. I had always taken a bit of stick for being a Mod then a scooterist, but most of it was pretty light-hearted. We were all 17, or 18 or older and most of the others were learning or had learnt to drive. One of them, Steve, had come to the disco for the first time in his own car. He had nothing but scathing comments for scooter riders.

'They ride in packs,' he said, 'What's that all about?'

I tried to explain based on Dave's descriptions of going to a scooter rally, but the truth was that I didn't have an argument because I had never done it myself, I had always ridden alone. I did wonder how riding with a group of mates changed things. Probably they had to be good mates too. I wasn't sure how I would feel riding with people I had only just met.

'You're a lot safer in a car,' Steve argued. 'You can't fall off for one thing.'

'True,' I said, 'but either way you can't drink.' I looked pointedly at the pint he had in front of him. I'd found I had begun to drink much less now that I travelled everywhere by scooter. I had once tried driving after I'd drunk half a pint and quickly decided that it was not a good idea. Since then, I'd been trying to come up with imaginative soft drinks, fairly unsuccessfully since most bars existed solely to sell alcohol.

The college had nursing and secretarial students and so, for a change, I was at a do that was roughly equal boys and girls. Somehow that meant that I had to make more of an effort. I had considered putting a skirt on but it was too restrictive on a scooter so I stuck to my usual jeans. I did put on a bit more make-up though.

Our course apart, most of the others seemed to divide across the gender lines. Construction was boys, health was girls and so on. This meant that the disco was clearly divided into groups of girls and groups of boys. It was an improvement on school discos which usually attracted only a handful of very brave boys.

As far as I could see, there were only girls on the dance floor. This turned out to be because the DJ was playing mostly Wham and Bananarama. Many of the girls looked old before their time, I thought. They had sensible skirts and satiny blouses. They had handbags. I wondered if this

131

was what I was trying to say that I wasn't. There was quite a lot of shrieking and giggling and attempts to flirt with the boys who were loitering on around the edges of the dance floor.

When the DJ switched to Madness and the Specials, the girls moved off and the boys moved on. This was my sort of music. It was what I had listened to on a loop from the age of 14. I didn't dance though. The dance was energetic and very boisterous, with lots of arm pumping and foot stomping. June was in the middle of it somewhere. I admired her ability to avoid being labelled. No one seemed to hold the fact that she was a girl against her in the way that they did with me. Or was I just thinking too hard about it all?

I saw Ben with one of the satin blouse brigade. You couldn't blame him for trying I supposed and he was sensible to turn his attentions from anyone too closely related to the SeaDogs.

June came off the dance floor, exhausted from the dancing. She gulped her half pint down in one and sat down.

'So, have you thought any more about Yarmouth yet?' she asked.

'Ben says I can ride up with him if I want,' I told her.

'Yarmouth?' said Steve, who was sitting on my other side, 'you're not planning to drive to Yarmouth on your scooter are you? You'll never make it.'

He didn't sound concerned, just certain that such a thing wasn't possible.

'What makes you say that?' I asked.

'Well, it must be, what, about a hundred miles and you can only go, let's say, twenty miles an hour, so allowing for fag and loo breaks, it's going to take you about six or seven hours. By the time you get there, it'll be time to go home again. You'll miss all the rocker-bashing.' He remained convinced that I was a Mod and that the purpose of rallies was to fight rockers on the beaches.

'I don't go twenty miles an hour.'

'Oh sorry, ten then so it'll take you twice as long, you'd better start now.'

'Look,' I said, 'I can go at least fifty.'

He grinned as if his point was made.

Steve's comments just made me determined to get to Yarmouth. I wanted the patch and the photos to prove that I'd made it. Not that I expected him to be impressed.

I told Ben that I was coming with him and arranged a time and place to meet on the Friday afternoon.

But then Dad said that he had a works do on the Friday evening and he wanted us all to attend, no excuses. So I was going to have to go on my own on the Saturday or not at all. I decided to make the trip anyway and phoned Ben and arranged to meet him at the campsite at lunchtime.

The works do was at the hall where I did most of my waitressing. It was a buffet though so I wasn't called on to work. Dad, Mum and Julia had got dressed up in their best gear and even I made an effort after Julia lent me one of her dresses. I was surprised that she had agreed since we were not the best of friends and hadn't been since I started

133

secondary school and ruined her carefully constructed reputation. These days she was everything I thought that I disliked. She had a steady job: a girl's job in a florists and a steady boyfriend called Barry. She was forever trying to get him to go and look at rings with her. We didn't spend much time together.

But as we sat down that evening we discovered that actually we had quite a bit in common. She admitted to me that she wasn't sure whether she had made the right decisions and was wondering about going back to college.

'I mean floristry's only something you do if you've got your own shop and I can't see me ever wanting to run my own shop,' she said.

'But you and Barry are going to get married and have kids aren't you? You won't work after that, will you?'

'I'm not sure I want kids, well not yet anyway.'

'That's the first sensible thing I've heard you say in three years,' said Mum who had been listening in on our conversation.

We both looked at her questioningly. Surely Mum wasn't going to come out against having kids? It was what she did, it was what she was.

'Look,' she said, 'when I was young, if you didn't get married by the time you were 23 you were considered an old maid. Relatives would talk about you as being on the shelf and your mother would worry about what was wrong with you. But this is the 1980s. Times have changed. I'm not saying don't get married and have kids but don't make it the first thing you do. If you do, you'll make it the only thing you do. Do you know how old I am?'

'Forty-one' we chorused.

'Forty-one. Exactly,' she said. 'And already you two don't need me anymore and in a few years you'll have left completely. What am I going to do then? I haven't got any skills, no one will employ me.'

'Have more kids?' said Dad hopefully. She shot him a look.

'Well I don't know, Mum. What do you want to do?' I asked. I had never given a thought to the idea that Mum might not be happy keeping house, that she might be bored on her own at home. She did a bit of volunteering of some sort and she had her knitting.

'Well, this is going to sound silly,' she began, 'but I'd really like to travel, to see the world. I've never been further than France.'

'Really?' said Julia.

'Where do you want to go?' I asked.

'Well, South America, I thought, India, Africa. I'd like to go and help somewhere, do some volunteering.'

We all looked at her, trying to make sense of what she was saying. Dad was the first to speak:

'But that would take you away for months! Who's would look after me?'

'You know, you can look after yourself,' she said gently. 'I'm not looking to go away forever. I'm just sick of looking at the same four walls every day, I want some new experiences.'

'But we're thinking of going to North Wales in the summer, you've never been there before,' he said.

'Exactly,' said Mum. 'Look I'm not getting into an argument here. I'm just telling you what I'd like to do, that's all, not what I will do.'

'You know, Mum. I think you should go,' said Julia. Annie can keep an eye on Dad. And maybe I'll come with you.'

'You know,' said Dad, 'maybe I'll come too.'

'Now that would be nice,' said Mum, 'but we'll have to sell the house to pay for it.'

I just looked at them all. I couldn't believe what I was hearing. It was one thing for me to be thinking of looking for work abroad but quite another for the rest of my family to decide to up sticks. I felt disorientated, lost. Didn't any of them care about me? Mum must have seen my face. She reached over and gave me a hug.

'Don't worry; we won't leave you on your own. You could come with us. How about we sell up, buy a camper van and all go and see the world?'

'What would we do when we got back?' I asked.

'Well maybe we won't come back. Maybe we'll find somewhere we want to be and stay.'

I tried to enjoy the rest of the evening. There were a few silly games that Julia and I got involved in, pretending we were ten again. Part of me wanted to show Mum how much I still needed her and maybe I could do that by making her think I was still a child. Julia seemed energized by the idea, though.

'Machu Pichu, I want to see,' she told me, 'Cuzco.' I had no idea what she was talking about. The DJ began to play some cheesy pop and Mum came up to dance. She and Julia were getting all giggly so I left them to it and went and sat with Dad. He was looking a bit glum.

'Do you really want to go, Dad?'

'Well, you know Annie,' he said, 'I'm happy with the ways things are. I like my job. We've got enough money for nice food and we go to the pictures and get away somewhere in the summer. I don't really want to upset all that. But, also, I love your Mum and I don't want her to be unhappy, so we have to find some way to make her happy.'

'It doesn't have to mean selling the house though does it? Where would I go?'

'I don't know, love. You are growing up though. Pretty soon you won't need us anymore.'

I couldn't imagine not needing my parents. They were Mum and Dad, capital M, capital D. That was their role. I might not need them for the day-to-day stuff but I did need to know they were still there.

'Perhaps you could save up for a two week cruise or something, maybe that would be enough for her,' I said to Dad hopefully.

'Yes. I'll try it, shall I?' he replied.

When I got up the next morning it was raining, hard.

'Is it going to be like this all day?' I asked Mum.

'I think so. Look you don't have to go do you? Why don't you stay here? We're going to the library to see what they've got in travel guides.'

'No, Mum, I can't. I've arranged to meet Ben and I've no way of letting him know, if I don't go.'

Well, I'm not keen you know.'

No, I wanted to say, and I'm not keen with you deciding to head off out into the world without a second glance. But I didn't. I packed all my stuff on the back of my scooter and tried to protect it from the rain as best as I could with plastic bags. Then I put on my cold and wet weather gear. I had two pairs of socks, a pair of leggings, jeans and over-trousers. I had a thermal vest, two t shirts, a jumper, a jacket and a parka. I had a scarf and two pairs of gloves. When I was ready I could hardly walk.

'At least if you fall off, you'll bounce,' said Julia, reverting to her usual sarcastic nature. I stuck two fingers up at her, but it wasn't clear due to the amount of clothing I had on, I could have been waving cheerfully.

I set off in the driving rain, heading east which seemed to be the direction that the wind was coming from. I had arranged to meet Ben in Yarmouth at 1.30pm. That gave me three and a half hours to cover a hundred miles.

Even before I had reached the main road I could feel that the rain had worked its way through the eyelets of my boots and into my socks. It was also dripping off my helmet onto my neck and down my back. I thought about turning back, but that seemed like giving in so I carried on, wiping away the rain from my face every so often and stretching out my fingers to stop them seizing up.

Once on the A12, I kept close to the edge of the road, not feeling safe out in the middle. Cars were shooting past and spraying me as they went. Some of them even seemed to be doing it on purpose.

I passed a roadside café that had scooters parked outside it. I felt really lonely making the journey on my own and couldn't bring myself to enter a place where I might be stared at as being a bit odd for being on my own and so I carried on. After a while though, I realised that I should have stopped to use the loos. There was no way I was going to reach Yarmouth without needing to stop. After too many miles and just when I was feeling that I wasn't going to make it I saw a sign for parking with toilets up ahead. I pulled in.

There was no one else in the lay-by. I used the facilities, peeling off the soggy layers of clothing as best I could. The long ride out in the elements had given me the shivers. There was nothing I could do about them and there was no way that I was going to be able to warm up where I was. I was going to have to keep going. At least it had almost stopped raining. I went to kick start my scooter but it wouln't go. It sounded as if it was never going to go again. I sat down on a wall, defeated. Every part of me seemed to be dripping and I still could not help shivering.

I wondered about flagging down a passing motorist, or waiting for a scooter to pass but neither idea appealed. I still hadn't made a decision about what to do when someone pulled up on a motorbike. He was a big bloke kitted out in full leathers. He took off his helmet to reveal a beard and long hair tied back in a ponytail. He looked at me shivering.

'Are you okay?' he asked. I seemed to have that question asked of me so many times. Usually I said yes, not wanting to cause anyone any bother, but this time I said no.

'What's up?' he asked.

'I can't get my scooter started again.'

'I'm not surprised. Bloody hairdryer. Do you want me to have a look at it for you?'

'Yes please,' I said, wetly.

He tried everything I tried and then treating it very roughly, managed to bump start it. He had a ride around the lay-by on it before bringing it back to me.

'Hmm,' he said, 'quite a laugh really, I've never ridden one before. You ought to dress more sensibly though.' He indicated his own waterproof exterior.

'I know, I expect I'll dry off by Monday,' I said.

He handed the running scooter over to me and I climbed astride it, squelching as I sat down.

'Thank you,' I said. I really was grateful.

I set off again, still shivering.

Somewhere near Ipswich, I saw some diversion signs that seemed to be relevant to me. I followed them, confidently at first, but soon appeared to be on a new road. More importantly, a new road that did not seem to have any other traffic on it. Since my usual response to being lost was to carry on riding and hope for the best, that is what I did. This didn't stop me imagining the road running out unexpectedly with me flying gracefully off the end. Still, if it was anything like Quadrophenia, the scooter would go flying off the end and I would be nowhere to be seen. All very enigmatic.

The road seemed to be cut through large fields and I couldn't even see any houses on the surrounding land. Then, unexpectedly, the land dropped away beneath the road and I was on a bridge that crossed a river. I still hadn't passed any traffic and none had passed me. I slowed down and then stopped, parking next to the barriers. Taking off my helmet, I leaned over the balustrade and surveyed the landscape. I seemed to be above an estuary as the river was widening behind me. I crossed the road to look to see where it went. It went to the sea; that was clear as the ground fell away and the water widened out into a blue grey expanse that seemed to stretch away forever. The skies were clearing a little now and as I stood there, the sun broke through and shone on the shrubs and grass that covered one of the riverbanks.

It didn't take much, I thought, to brighten my mood. A bit of sun, and anything was possible. I had made the right decision to make this journey and I would have a good weekend. I wondered if this was what Mum was hoping for really, a bit of sun warming her face, a feeling that she could do the things she wanted rather than doing the things

141

everyone else wanted. If so, I thought that a two week cruise wasn't going to be enough.

Now I had to decide whether to carry on along this new road, or play it safe and retrace my steps hoping to pick up my original route. With the sun still shining, I decided to be brave and see where the road took me.

I had forgotten that the scooter had not restarted earlier, but, like me, it must have been drying out a bit and it started first kick.

I carried on along the still empty road and almost without me noticing it we merged back on to the busy route heading to the coast.

As I approached Yarmouth there were actually signs pointing to way to the rally campsite. I joined on the end of a large group of scooter riders, none of whom seemed to have noticed that they had gained one extra.

I arrived twenty minutes before I was due to meet Ben. I parked up and set about removing some of my outer layers of clothing, hanging them over and across the scooter until it looked like a child's den made out of the contents of a dressing up box. I got a few funny looks but I was past caring.

One-thirty came and went without any sign of Ben. I began to wonder if he had forgotten about me or if one of us had got the time wrong. Then I began to wonder if he had even made it to Yarmouth.

I waited until past 2 o'clock, then I decided to have a look around the campsite. I tidied up my stuff and left my scooter where it was so he would know I was around somewhere if he did show up.

The campsite was on a racecourse and the tents were spread out across the areas outside of the track. I knew it would be an impossible task to locate one person in this great sea of people and tents and scooters. Everywhere was sodden but it did not look as though the rain had put many people off. Many of the tents looked as though the rain had soaked right through them. Some had soggy items of clothing draped across the top. There didn't seem to be anywhere dry to sit and so everyone was using their scooters as makeshift chairs. Quite a few were sat two-up which looked no less uncomfortable stationary as it did on the road.

I was looking for anyone I might know or recognise from the Red Cow. With a shudder I remembered John and hoped I would not bump into him on my way round. I wouldn't have minded seeing Bill again though.

Feeling hungry I went in search of the food stalls. There was one selling soup which was a welcome change from the usual burger fare. I sat down with my cup of tomato soup and a roll. I had barely started on it though when I heard someone say my name.

'Annie?' I looked up, it was Sam, with some of the Sessex Girls. 'It is Annie isn't it?' I nodded. I was relieved to at least see someone I knew.

'Are you here on your own?' she asked.

'Yes. I've just got here, I was supposed to be meeting Ben at the entrance but he hasn't shown up.'

'No, well he won't. He's had an accident.' She looked quite tearful.

'Oh no. Is he okay?'

'We don't know.' Sam had been standing up, blocking the light but she took the chair next to me.

'Sam, we'll get you some soup, okay?' one of the other girls said as they wandered off to the stall.

I had gone cold again. 'Do you know what happened?'

'Yes. He had a few drinks last night and then about midnight or so, decided to go for a ride down the front. Apparently he didn't stop at a junction and collided with a car.'

'How did you know about it?'

'Karen and Suzy were coming back from town and they saw the ambulance and everything and realised that it was Ben. They had taken him away before we got there though. I went to the local hospital this morning and they said they've moved him to Norwich because they've got better facilities there.'

'Oh.' I didn't know what to say.

'Sorry. It must be a shock.' I nodded.

'Yes. That would explain why he wasn't there to meet me. What happened to his scooter?' I did really care what happened to his scooter, I was just looking for something to say.

144

'The police have taken it I think, but Karen said it was a bit of a wreck.'

'Should I go to Norwich do you think?'

'I think his family will be there by now.'

'Oh. Yes. Of course.' I was letting my soup go cold.

'Are you really on your own then?'

'Yes, it looks like it.'

'You could hang out with us if you like. I'm sure the others won't mind.'

I was really grateful for the offer. 'Yes, thank you.'

The other girls came over. 'You don't mind if Annie hangs out with us, do you?' Sam asked them.

'No,' said Karen, 'the more the merrier. Were you supposed to be meeting Ben?'

I nodded. 'I saw him,' she continued, 'he looked in a pretty bad way. He hit a Merc and you're always going to come off worst if you hit one of those. It shook us all up.'

'Have you got any stuff with you?' Sam asked.

'Yes, it's with my scooter. I left it at the entrance in case Ben showed up.' I was on the verge of tears.

'Well, look, I'll show you where we are and you can bring it through.'

Sam led the way through the tents to their little patch and I used the walk to try and get a grip on myself. There was a spare bit of grass where I could squeeze my tent on to. I brought everything over and the girls helped me put the thing up. There

145

were five of them altogether, Sam, Karen, Suzy and two girls I recognised but did not know. They introduced themselves as Sarah and Andrea. All of them were surprisingly friendly and chatty.

'It's a good job we found you,' said Andrea, 'We had five people and two tents, one of which got completely waterlogged so we ended up with all of us in one, which was a bit of a squash. With yours we'll have six people and two tents so we'll have a bit more room. If you don't mind that is.'

'No, I don't mind.'

'Good, we'll sort it out later.'

Chapter Twelve

As the evening approached, the girls decided they were going into town.

'They've put a bus on for us,' said Suzy, 'can you believe it?' We walked up to the entrance and sure enough, there was a double decker waiting with 'Scooter rally special' written on a sign in the front window.

'Very thoughtful,' I said.

'Keeps the scooters off the road, more like,' said Andrea.

'They sold tickets to the all-nighter,' Suzy told me on the way 'and they all sold out, so we missed out on that. So we're just heading for the pub we went to last night.'

'It's got music and a dance floor though,' added Andrea.

I felt I owed the girls something so I bought the first round of drinks and we settled ourselves into a corner. To begin with I mostly just listened to their conversation, but after a while, once the alcohol had worked its way into my system, I got more talkative.

'So how do you get on, on these rallies, being all girls?' I asked Suzy.

'How do you mean?'

'Well are there any other all-girl clubs? You must stand out. Do you get lots of comments?'

147

'Well, I don't think we're unique,' Suzy answered,' I know of a couple of other all-girl clubs up North, but, yes, there aren't many of us and yes, we do get comments.'

'Mostly they think we're all lesbians,' added Sam.

'Which you're not,' I said.

'Well some of us are,' said Sarah. 'Me and Andrea are, though we're not an item.'

'Oh,' I said. I was about to say that they didn't look like lesbians, because they both had stylish hair and good make up, but actually I didn't know what lesbians looked like or whether I should be able to identify them by sight.

'It's not that unusual, you know,' said Andrea. 'You're not threatened by it are you?'

'No,' I answered, 'it doesn't make any difference to me. I don't even know what I am.'

'Have you ever been attracted to a girl?' Sarah asked.

'I don't think so, although there was a girl on a bus once who quite fascinated me and I never really knew why.'

'Well you'd know by now, if you were or not.'

'I've never had a boyfriend *or* a girlfriend though.'

'How old are you?' asked Suzy.

'Seventeen.'

'Seventeen, and you've never had a boyfriend? That's a bit unusual. But you are still quite young,' Suzy said.

'Yes, well I had a few fumbles at school, a bit of a kiss and a cuddle, that sort of thing. But nothing has ever come of it.'

'So you've never had sex, of any sort?'

'I shook my head.'

'Wow.' Everyone looked shocked.

'But Ben . . .?' asked Sam.

'He's just a friend.' I was going to add that he wasn't the sort of person I would want to have a shag with, but remembering what had happened at Morecambe, decided to leave that unsaid.

I felt I wanted to tell Sam that Dave had taken me to the football, but I didn't know how to approach the subject. She introduced it for me though.

'I heard that you'd been seeing a bit of Dave,' she said.

'Well, not really. He took me to a football match, that's all. Do you mind?'

'No,' she replied. 'Well, that's not true. I do mind a little bit. But Dave and I had it coming for ages. We were supposed to be boyfriend and girlfriend but we hardly ever saw each other. He was always with his mates and I was always with mine. Then I had the idea that we needed to do some more stuff together, so I made him come horse-riding. My sister works at the stables, you see. And, well, you know how that turned out.'

'He didn't blame you for his broken arm, did he?'

'Not obviously, but underneath it all, I could tell he thought it was my fault.'

'Oh.'

149

'I wish that we'd ended it all a bit more sensibly, that's all. And that was my fault. I got angry and hurt two people, Dave and Ben.'

'Is Dave here, do you know?' I asked. 'Did he get his cast off?'

'Yes, all the SeaDogs are here somewhere. We saw them at the campsite yesterday, didn't we, Suzy?'

Suzy nodded. 'Yes, you should see Lance's scooter. He's finally got it finished and it looks brilliant. He's had a paintjob done and it's all green with trees on it.'

'That sounds different.'

I had not thought about Lance for a while. After not hearing from him or seeing him after Morecambe, and then being invited out by Dave, I had pushed him to the back of my mind a bit. But talking about him made me think of the way he held my hand when we walked back to the car and how he had planted that little kiss on my nose. There was something about those actions that made my tummy turn over. There was something very gentle and sensitive about him, something that you wouldn't guess from looking at him.

Some of the girls made a move to the dance floor, and I went with them, still thinking about Lance. It wasn't long until we were surrounded by scooter boys, all doing a bit of showing off with their moves. I don't think any of them thought any of us were lesbians but Sarah and Andrea made their sexuality clear with the way they were dancing. This only got the lads more interested.

The pub seemed to have a late licence and we ended up weaving our way out of there around midnight.

Back at the campsite, Karen unearthed a half bottle of vodka which she added to a bottle of coke and the six of us piled into one of the tents and passed the bottle round.

Inevitably the talk turned to Ben's accident.

'We've been quite lucky, up till now,' Sam said. 'Salty wrote off his baby scoot a few years ago, but that's all the accidents we've had within the Red Cow lot.'

'Who's come off their scooter though?' Andrea asked. Everyone apart from me and Suzy put their hands up.

'Wow,' I said, surprised.

'You can't call yourself a proper scooterist until you've come off at least once,' Andrea said.

'And you've got to have the scars to prove it too,' Karen added, rolling up her trousers to show us the marks from her injuries.

Eventually we decided to call it a night. I got up to go to my tent and invited anyone who wanted to, to join me. Suzy and Sarah both decided that they would. Sarah crawled in miserably trailing her sleeping bag.

'It's still wet at the bottom' she said, showing us the corner which was dripping water on the grass.

'Well mine's dry,' said Suzy. 'How about yours, Annie?'

I nodded. My packing for the journey had managed to be pretty effective and the sleeping bag had stayed in a usable condition.

'So how about if we unzip them and have one underneath and one on top between us and plug the gaps with jumpers?' suggested Suzy.

And so we settled down, the three of us sharing bedding and body warmth. I was in the middle and lay awake for hours listening to the gentle breathing of the other girls. Had I been told that this was how I was going to end my day at the beginning of it I wouldn't have believed it.

I must have fallen asleep eventually. When I awoke, I was lying on my side, pinned down by an arm thrown across my waist from behind. It was Sarah, who was snoring gently in my ear. It felt nice, her arm was light and yet comforting. Something made me take hold of her hand and pull it closer to me. I fell asleep again. Much later I woke up, seemingly disturbing Sarah in the process. We had not changed positions and she seemed surprised that we were so closely entwined.

I still had my arm over hers, so I let it go.

'Sorry,' she said.

'It's alright. It was nice,' I said.

And it was, although I didn't think it made me fancy her. I thought I was just looking for some comfort.

Our voices woke Suzy and we all pulled on our boots and coats and made for the loos. These were proper loos built for the racecourse customers and so we were able to wash with hot water.

'What are you doing today?' I asked as we queued for coffee and bacon rolls.

'There's an all-dayer on, in one of the buildings here somewhere,' Sarah replied, 'so we'll probably go there.'

When we got back to the tents some lads from a neighbouring tent had joined the others. Everywhere had dried out enough for us to sit on plastic bags or coats on the ground and so we sat around chatting for a while. The lads brought over a calor gas ring and we boiled up water for coffee and warmed up beans which we ate out of the pan.

The boys seemed to have a ready supply of cannabis. I was intrigued as I had never come into contact with any drugs before. A girl I knew at school claimed that the sixth form parties were awash with them and one of the boys on my college course made a habit of coming in late looking boggle-eyed and telling tales of hot knives and foil none of which I could make sense of. But I supposed I had a too innocent looking face as no one had thought to offer any to me.

The lads crumbled the stuff they'd brought into cigarette papers mixed up with loose tobacco. They passed it around generously. Both Sam and Sarah said no thanks. I knew that I should have said no but I did want to try it. I also wanted to look as if I knew what I was doing and tried very hard to inhale the smoke without coughing. I failed and was found out straight away.

'Was that your first toke?' asked the lad who had passed it to me. I nodded, unable to speak.

'Oh well, take it easy then.'

I had a couple more goes when it came round again. I began to feel a bit light-headed and after a while I did feel more relaxed. Things seemed to move into a softer focus. I was quite happy where I was, but after a while everyone seemed to want to move on, so I followed them.

As we were weaving through the tents on the way to the hall where we thought the all-dayer was, I saw a green scooter with a landscape view painted on the side panels and a single willow tree on the front panel. When I saw Dave's scooter parked up alongside it, I knew it had to be Lance's. The painted view looked familiar somehow. It took me a while to realise that it looked a little like the meadow we had stopped at on the way to Morecambe. That place was obviously really important to him although the scooter gave no clue as to why.

There hadn't been anyone round the scooters, so I wondered if they were at the all-dayer. I did want to see Lance again, although I didn't know what I was going to say when I did.

I didn't say anything to anyone for ages. The all-dayer was heaving and I lost myself in the crowd and in the music.

There was a succession of bands. I danced to each with intensity, but once each song was finished, I instantly forgot it and concentrated on the next. At some point I realised that my cheeks were sore because I was smiling so much. If anyone spoke to me I just smiled back at them and nodded. I was in a crowd of people and yet utterly alone. For a while I felt safe and secure, somehow outside of time.

After what seemed like hours, I felt exhausted and looked for somewhere to sit down for a rest. I ended up sitting on a bench outside the hall. The campsite was laid out in front of me; all the colours of the rainbow were there, tents of orange and yellow, scooters of red and blue, people in green and black moving around and through them.

Someone came and sat down beside me. It was Lance.

'Hello,' he said, 'you looked as though you were having a good time in there.'

'I was.' I didn't know I was being watched. 'I saw your scooter.'

'What do you think?'

'It looks good,' I replied. 'Interesting picture.'

'Thanks, a bit different from the usual, I thought. My dad would like it.'

'I rode up on mine,' I said.

'Did you? Who did you come with?'

'No one. I came on my own. I was supposed to meet Ben here.'

'Oh yes?' he sounded suspicious, but also as though he hadn't heard about the accident.

'Yes, but he wasn't there, he came off his scooter on Friday night.'

'Oh.' Lance stopped short. 'I heard someone had copped it, I didn't know it was Ben.'

'He didn't cop it, he's in Norwich hospital, or so I heard.'

'Who told you?'

'Sam. She went up to the hospital yesterday morning.'

'Oh well, she should know better than me then.'

'I hope so.'

'Is that who you're with then?' Lance asked after a moment.

'Sam? Yes, and the others.' Lance made a face.

'What do you mean? They were really kind to me. I'd have been on my own otherwise; I'd probably have gone home again.'

'Yes, but Andrea and Sarah are into each other aren't they?'

'Well, no, they're not actually. But why should it matter if they were?'

He shrugged. 'I don't suppose it does. It's just what blokes say, isn't it? Just make sure they don't try any funny business on you.'

'You're always trying to protect me, aren't you?'

'Yeah, well, it's just . . . you see so many girls sleeping with anyone and everyone. Perhaps I think you should be different.'

'Why me?'

'You haven't been . . .' he seemed to be trying to find the right word, 'spoilt.'

'Oh. I see. And nor will I be with you looking out for me. I will remain forever unspoilt.' I said this dramatically.

'Well,' he said in response, 'you can do what you want, I suppose.'

156

'Thank you. I will.'

Lance stood up. 'I'm going back in,' he said.

I decided to go back to the tents to see if the girls had returned there.

'At least,' Lance said to me as I left, 'it should be right, shouldn't it? Not in a tent, or on the beach or somewhere with loads of people around.'

I turned to look at him. He had annoyed me, he was more down on me than Dad. I couldn't see what he was trying to save me from. But he did have a point. You would only have a first time once.

I stood there, my hands in my pockets, hugging myself, he made me feel so alone as if there were no one who would be good enough to make it right.

'Yeah,' I said, 'maybe I'll find someone soon. Before I get old.'

Lance stood up. He moved towards me and then stopped.

'Yes. I hope you will,' he said, before turning away. I watched him go back into the hall. He didn't look round.

Chapter Thirteen

Sam and Suzy were back at the tents when I got there. The others had gone for a ride out along the coast. The three of us took the bus into town again and spent a night similar to the one before. I had a good time but was tired from the dancing and the lack of sleep. The other girls joined us later and once we were all together, Sam said:

'Annie, we wondered if you would like to join the Sessex Girls? We talked it over, because we all had to agree.'

'We are all founder members, you see,' said Andrea. 'We've never had anyone new join before.'

'What would it mean?'

'Well, not much really,' said Sam. 'We don't have any proper meetings and we don't have any patches or badges. But we do hang out together and we do go to rallies together.'

'And you could write Sessex Girls S.C. on the back of your parka if you wanted,' said Karen.

'Oh well, in that case, then, yes please,' I said. 'Thank you for asking me.'

I really was happy that they had asked me and that all of them had agreed. I had always been outside of things and finally I felt as though I was on the inside. Even better I was with a group of girls who had made a success of being in a boys' world. I felt empowered as if there was strength in numbers.

Back at the tents, the third one had finally dried out and we split into twos. Sarah came in mine again but this time we had our own bags and we slept apart. We hadn't talked any more about waking up in each other's arms. If it had been a boy's arm I had found around me I would have been questioning his motive but I didn't feel that I needed to with Sarah.

In the morning we took down the tents and got ready to leave. As I had been made a proper member of the group, I didn't feel I needed to ask if it was okay if I rode back with them, I just assumed that it would be.

All the girls had work tomorrow and so we set off before lunch in order to make it home about mid-afternoon. As we left the campsite we joined a sea of scooters all heading out of town. Most of us were going as fast as the leaders but there were a few nipping in and out of spaces in the pack.

As we reached road junctions, some groups turned off in different directions and eventually there were only the six of us left. We rode in single file, averaging about fifty miles an hour. A few cars went past and some of them bibbed their horns in a friendly manner. It was all so different from my journey up. I didn't see a diversion and we didn't follow my empty road. I didn't even see us crossing a river. I was beginning to think that I had imagined it.

When we reached town, Sam led us to the Red Cow and we all parked up and said our goodbyes. I arranged to meet them at the next soul night. I rode home happily and when I got back, even though it was only tea-time, I went straight to bed and slept until morning.

The next morning I had college. Mum was in the kitchen when I went down for breakfast.

'Is everything alright?' she asked me.

'Yes, why shouldn't it be?'

'You had that Lance come round last night.'

'I did? Why didn't you wake me?'

'Well I did come up but you were fast asleep and I didn't want to disturb you.'

'Did he say why he came round?'

'No, I did ask if he wanted to leave a message, but he said he'd catch up with you, so I left it at that.'

'Oh.'

On the way to college I wondered why Lance had come round. I wondered if he had news about Ben. I was desperate to get to college to see June to find out what she knew.

It turned out that she hadn't heard anything about the accident at all and was upset to hear the news, particularly since I had so few details. She was already down about having spent the weekend on her own at home. I sensed actually that she hadn't spent the weekend alone in the way she said although I couldn't work out who she might have spent it with.

She tried phoning Ben's parents from a pay phone but got no reply.

'Well he must be still alive,' she reasoned, 'or his parents would be back at the house.'

'Unless they are back at the house and just aren't answering the phone,' I added.

The day got worse for June when I told her about being invited to join the Sessex Girls.

'Who am I going to hang out with now, if you're going to be with those lot?' she asked.

'You could hang out with us,' I offered.

'Do you think they'd want me to join?' she asked.

'Why not?' I answered, although I wasn't sure that they would.

The next day June came to college breathless with news. She'd gone round to Ben's house and, finding it deserted, gone round to the neighbours who had been asked to look after the family's cats.

'He's in a coma,' she said. He's been in it since Friday and his parents and Tom are sitting with him, trying to wake him up.

I felt sick. I didn't know much about comas but I knew that they weren't good.

'Aren't they supposed to play his favourite music or something?' I asked.

'I think so. Shall we go up at the weekend, do you think?' June asked. 'I think I need to do something positive if I can.'

We took the train up to Norwich on Saturday. June had managed to get a message through to Ben's parents and they were expecting us. We weren't prepared for the sight of him though. I had been to visit people in hospital in a ward before but I had never been in Intensive Care.

I had always thought of Ben as being small, but laying in bed attached to various machines, he looked tiny. He had bandages around his head but even with these on we could see that they had shaved his hair as there were none of his usual curls escaping below.

'I don't understand,' I said to his dad, 'surely his helmet would have protected his head.'

'Apparently, he wasn't wearing one,' his dad replied grimly. I had dressed carefully so as to look less like a scooter girl in case his parents thought I had something to do with it. Tom, similarly, looked as though he was looking to blend in. His mum said that she had tried to persuade Tom to go back to work but that he had refused. He looked washed out and barely spoke to us. When I went to get some drinks though I came back to find Tom talking angrily to June in a corner of the corridor.

We only stayed for a short while. There was clearly nothing we could do although Ben's parents thanked for coming. On the way out, June produced a cassette tape which she gave to his mum and asked if they could play it to him sometime.

On the train back, June was very subdued. I asked her what Tom had been talking to her about.

'Apparently, according to him, it's all my fault. Ben's accident that is.'

'How does he figure that one out?'

'Well, he says that he would have been at Yarmouth if he hadn't lost his licence and he would have stopped him riding drunk. And the reason he lost his licence was because he was caught giving me a lift when he wasn't supposed to.' June looked close to tears, which wasn't like her at all.

'That doesn't sound very fair,' I said.

'I know,' she replied. 'I know that he's being really unreasonable really, but he was so vicious, so angry, he made me think that he was right.' She sniffed, she really was crying but I didn't want to let her know that I had noticed. I turned to look out of the window.

'You know,' she said after a while, 'I don't set out to hurt anybody, but sometimes I do, just because of how I am. What do I have to do to make sure that doesn't happen?'

I didn't know what to say in reply. How could I tell her that I thought that she was careless sometimes and that sometimes that could lead to problems and people being hurt in different ways. I couldn't, because what I admired about her was her carelessness.

'You know,' I said in the end, 'people have to be responsible for themselves. Ben shouldn't have ridden drunk, Tom should have told you that he couldn't give you a lift. It wasn't your fault.' June nodded but she did not look convinced. She seemed to have had the wind taken out of her sails.

On Monday at college she went around as if she was in a dream and on Tuesday she didn't show up at all. This was a mistake because it was the day we were allocated our work experience placements and she ended up with Debenhams' coffee shop.

I got Crendell's staff canteen, which didn't sound much better except it would give me a chance to see both Lance and Dave.

I saw them both at the Red Cow on the Wednesday night. I couldn't persuade June to come so I parked up with the Sessex Girls and spent the evening with them.

I hadn't seen or spoken to Dave since we had parted after the football so I didn't really know what to say to him. I settled for asking if he enjoyed Yarmouth. He said he had, but the talk was all about Ben. I was the only person there who had been to see him so I had plenty of attention as everyone wanted the latest news, even though none of it was good. I wanted to speak to Lance to ask him why he had come round to my house but he seemed to stand on the edge of the group when I told everyone about Ben and then I saw him move swiftly away.

He spent the evening in a group of SeaDogs who remained aloof and unapproachable. I kept tabs on him though. I sneaked a glance over at him every so often and once or twice I thought I caught a head movement as he looked quickly away. He left quite early and after that I felt as though I might just as well leave too, even though I was enjoying the music and the girls were good company. Sam said that there was another rally in a few weeks' time, somewhere in the Midlands and asked if I was going to join them. I wasn't sure as I hadn't worked much in the past couple of months and money was a bit tight.

It was nearly mid-summer and so when I rode home at the end of the evening, the sun seemed to have only just gone down. The dusk was beautiful to ride through and I only had a couple of layers of clothes on which was liberating after the hundreds of layers I had worn over the winter. I felt free and as though anything was possible. I made a wish to whoever or whatever might be above and beyond us that Ben would pull through.

June kept up with the news about Ben. The following week both Tom and his dad returned home as both had to be back at work.

'Tom came to see me,' June told me, 'and he apologised for what he said at the hospital.'

'What did you say?' I asked.

'Not much, I wasn't going to make him feel bad. Ben hasn't improved at all, he said. Although I think the only improvement on a coma is being out of it. All or nothing, you might say.'

'So are you friends again?'

'I think so, he and his dad are going back up again on Sunday and they're going to take me with them.'

'Are you going to be back in time for Debenhams?'

'Oh. Yes, probably. But who cares if I'm not? I don't think I can stand a whole week of cleaning tables and serving up teacakes.'

I was quite looking forward to my week out. It would make a change from sitting in classrooms.

Mum hadn't spoken any more about her desire to travel but she had received a few thick letters that she took away to read in private. It made me sad to see her go, lost in her own plans, although I knew I should be pleased for her.

She kept asking me if I had seen Lance again and seemed hopeful that my week working in Crendell's would bring some progress on our non-existent relationship.

I had to be at the canteen at 7am on Monday. I rode in by scooter and left it in a section of car park marked out for motorbikes. As I was parking up, a man arrived on a Suzuki motorbike. He looked me over.

'Are you the work experience?' he asked.

'In the canteen?' I asked. 'Yes.'

He stuck his hand out and introduced himself as Mike Grieve, the catering manager.

'Not another bloody scooter,' he said as we walked in. 'I don't know what the fascination is with them.'

He introduced me to the other canteen staff. 'Watch out,' he said, 'she's a Mod.'

'I'm not a Mod,' I argued. 'I'm a scooterist.' But no one was listening.

'You're not very smart for a Mod,' said Bob the kitchen porter. 'I thought you lot were supposed to dress smart.' I decided not to argue, it didn't seem worth it. It was easier to be a Mod for the week.

That first morning I was put to helping out with the food preparation. No one really needed my help but they found me jobs to do. I was bringing the food through to the serving area for lunchtime service when I heard Mike say: 'We've got one of your lot in this week.'

I thought he was talking about me and looked up to see that he was talking to someone through the counter. It was Lance who looked different out of his usual Army green and in blue overalls instead. I don't suppose I looked my normal self either though since I was dressed in chef's whites and a paper hat.

I waved and he nodded back and walked off with his tray of food over to a table with other blue-overalled staff. I looked to see if Dave was one of them but I couldn't see him. I didn't actually know what job Dave did. There were lots of different groups, most of the factory floor staff seemed to be in white coats or overalls, while the warehouse staff were blue. The office staff, in their own clothes, came in later than the others.

I thought I had missed Dave, but just as we were getting ready to clear up he came rushing in. He was wearing a shirt and tie.

'Sorry,' he said to Mike, 'I forgot the time.'

'You're lucky, we've got a portion of chilli left,' he replied. 'That, or a cheese and onion sandwich.'

'Oh, chilli then please,' Dave said.

He seemed to be looking around for someone. When he saw me, he smiled.

'I saw your scooter out the front,' he said. 'You didn't say you were coming to work here.'

'Just for the week,' I said.

'Work experience,' said Mike, 'which means we all get to put our feet up for a week. We like work experience round here.'

167

'I didn't know you worked in the office,' I said.

'Yes. Distribution. I arrange the lorry loads, make sure they go to the right places with the right stuff on them.'

'Oh. Sounds interesting.'

'Now why don't I think you mean that?'

Dave sat down on his own to eat his lunch. I began to clear the empty tables around him.

'Any news on Ben?' he asked.

'No. June went up to see him yesterday, I think. I haven't heard from her how it went yet. Last I heard there was no change.'

'It shakes you up doesn't it?' he said.

I nodded.

'Look, what time do you finish?'

'About three, I think, I've been here since seven.'

'Oh well, not to worry then, I'm here till five. I just thought I could take you for a coffee or something.'

'Another time, maybe.'

'Yes, we should sort something out.'

He got up holding his plate and cup. 'I'll clear these up for you.' He stopped and then, after thinking for a moment said 'What do you think of Salty?'

'Lance? I think . . . he's very . . . special, I suppose.' I couldn't find the right words to explain what I thought about him really, especially when explaining what I thought about him to Dave. I would have chosen a different word if I had been describing what I thought about him to June.

'Special?' Dave said. 'In a good way?'

'Yes, in a good way. I don't know why you are asking, but you can tell him that if you want.'

'Yes, okay.' I couldn't really tell what Dave thought of my reply. I wanted to tell him that I thought that he was special too, but in a different way, but I didn't know why he was asking about Lance and it might all have sounded a bit strange.

Recently I had been thinking about Dave and Lance and who I would prefer to go out with if either one of them asked me properly. There was something solid about Dave, reliable, honourable even. There was something there that I wanted to get close to. But Lance was the one who intrigued me. He was the one who made my stomach flip. There was a softness to him, that I didn't think he revealed to many people. I thought I had fallen a little bit in love with him although I wasn't about to admit that to anybody.

The next day I got to shadow Mike while he did his menu planning and food ordering and so did not see either Lance or Dave at lunchtime. I did wonder whether Dave would have told Lance what I had said, and if so whether he would respond in some way.

Mike was quick to pick up on the situation.

'So, you know those scooter lads, do you?' he asked in between sorting out his dry goods order.

'Yes, quite well.'

'Either of them your boyfriend?'

'No.'

'Do you want either of them to be your boyfriend? I could put a word in for you if you like.' He seemed to like meddling in other people's lives and I supposed I was a new challenge.

'No, it's okay, thanks. I think it would be better if you didn't.'

'Oh well, if you change your mind let me know, you've only got three more days of my services, though, you know.'

On Wednesday, I was put in charge of omelettes so was kept in the kitchen filling the orders as they came in. When lunch was over, Mike came over.

'There was a phone call for you earlier,' he said. 'Someone called June. She asked if you can go and see her at work when you've finished here.'

'Okay. Thanks,' I said. I wondered how she'd managed to find the number, it must have taken some doing so I thought it must be important.

When I finished at three, I decided to ride in to town and see what the news was. I could see that there was something on my scooter before I got there. It was a letter slid underneath the seat strap. The envelope was just addressed to Annie, written in careful neat handwriting . It was sealed. I wasn't going to open it then and there, it felt as though the whole factory was watching me, even though few windows opened out onto the car park. I put it in my bag to look at later.

Debenhams coffee shop was still very busy by the time I got there. June said it was the cream tea rush. Most of the customers seemed to be ladies of pension age, having a bit of a treat perhaps. Despite only having been there three days, June already seemed to have made herself at home and

170

was passing the time of day with anyone and everyone.

She didn't even see me come in. I had to call to her. When she did see me, she let out a whoop and, dropping her cloth, she came out from behind the counter.

'Can I just have a couple of minutes, Mary?' she called to someone who I took to be the supervisor.

'As long as it is just a couple of minutes,' Mary called back.

'How about if I buy a scone? Then you could be legitimately talking to a customer.' I suggested.

'I'll give you a scone, you don't need to buy one,' June said, ''there's not much in the way of stock control here.'

We stood over by the cleaning station while June told me the news.

'Ben's out of the coma,' she said. 'Yesterday evening. Tom came round about eleven to tell me. He was so happy.' I gave her a hug.

'So how is he?'

'Well, on the mend I think. I wanted to go straight up there, but they want to keep the number of visitors down for a bit. Tom said he'd let me know when they drop restrictions. I think it was my doing you know, I played that soul compilation on Sunday and reminded him he was missing the rally season.'

'June, if you want a good report, you better get back to work right now,' Mary shouted from behind the counter, 'Boyfriend out of a coma, or not.'

'Better go,' June said. 'I'll let you know if I get the word that we can go up there, okay?'

Chapter Fourteen

I felt relieved by the news that Ben was on the mend rather than out and out happy. I had kind of got used to the situation as it was, but to be on the other side of it felt good. I hoped there wasn't any lingering problems that would only be revealed when Ben started walking again or something.

The news had made me forget about the letter and it wasn't until after tea that I remembered it. I took my bag up to my room for some privacy.

My room was something of a mish-mash. When I was about ten, I had a friend with reasonably rich parents and she had Laura Ashley matching wallpaper and curtains. The idea the curtains could match the wallpaper seemed amazing to me and I badgered Mum until she found a cheap copy. My room was still papered the beige paper covered with brown and cream flowers that I had chosen. On my bed I had a Paddington Bear bedspread that, at the age of twelve, I had sworn I would still like five years later. I was wrong, I didn't. To try to hide some of this I had photocopied pictures of scooters and Mods out of library books and stuck them on the wall above lyrics from Quadrophenia that I had painstakingly copied out of the LP insert. It wasn't a room that I wanted to take anybody back to. I thought it made me look a bit weird.

Making sure the door was closed and that no one was moving about nearby and likely to burst in on me, I opened the envelope and slid out the letter. It was written on lined paper.

'Dear Annie,' I read, 'Dave has told me that he thinks you like me, based on a conversation that you had the other day. Well I have wanted to tell you that I like you for quite some time but do not seem to be able to. I came to see you after Yarmouth but your mum would not wake you up. So I am writing a letter instead. I hope you don't think this is cowardly. Would you like to meet sometime, just you and me. I could come to yours and we could find a pub near you. Any evening this or next week is okay for me. Let me know. Lance.'

He had added his phone number to the bottom of the letter.

I read it over several times. I knew that I did want to meet him. I was touched that he had gone to the effort of writing the letter and found somewhere to leave it. I did think that there was something cowardly about it but there was something quite sweet about it too. I wondered how to reply. I could leave a note on his scooter I supposed, but it would be braver to speak to him. I was going to have to speak to him, if we went out.

I wanted to tell him and Dave the good news about Ben anyway. I didn't want to wait until lunchtime and hope to catch him in the line. Something told me he might avoid the canteen if he hadn't heard from me anyway. So when we stopped for a break, I asked Mike, if it was okay if I went over to the warehouse.

'Plumped for Lance, have you?' he asked.

'Maybe,' I answered.

'Good choice, I think,' he replied, pointing me in the right direction.

I was very nervous walking over. Once inside the door, I realised that it wasn't going to be easy locating Lance. The warehouse was filled with rows and rows of pallets of soft drinks. There were a number of forklifts moving about and all the drivers wore the same overalls along with yellow hard hats. Inside a glass-fronted supervisor's office there was a middle-aged man on the phone. I hovered by the door, waiting until he had finished his call.

'Can I speak to Lance, please,' I said when he looked up.

'Yes. What about?' he asked.

'Oh.' I hadn't been expecting to explain myself to anyone else. 'Personal stuff, you know.'

The supervisor gave me a funny look. 'In the middle of work time?'

'It'll only take a minute.'

'Well make sure it does.'

He picked up a walkie-talkie-type machine and spoke into it.'

'Monkey Man, calling Monkey Man, you are needed in the office.'

He'll be over in a moment, said the man, leaving the office. I could see Lance walking over from the far side of the warehouse, taking his hard hat off on the way. I wondered why the manager had called him 'Monkey man'.

He came into the office, looking a little scared.

'I got your letter,' I said. I was talking quickly trying to get all the words I had practised out before I forgot them, 'and I wanted to say, yes, I would like to meet you and maybe Monday night would be a good time?' I had thought hard about what day to suggest. Friday was good but it was the next day which suggested that neither of us had anything much in the way of a social life. And the next Friday was the beginning of the next scooter rally. A weekday was good anyway because it was less pressure than a weekend night. In the end I had gone for Monday. 'Oh and Ben's out of his coma.' I added.

'Really?'

I wondered what he was saying 'Really?' to. The fact that I had agreed to go out with him or the fact that Ben was recovering.

'Yes,' I said in response.

'Good,' he said, 'Eight o'clock alright for you?'

I nodded.

'Better get back,' I said and moved to go past him to the door. He grabbed my hand as I passed and gave it a squeeze.

'Thank you,' he said. Then as I was on the way out, 'scooter or car?'

'Sorry?'

'Shall I pick you up by scooter or car?'

'Oh. Scooter, I think.' I had never ridden on the back of anyone's scooter before and had often wanted to try it.

Friday was my last day at Crendell's. I had enjoyed it and could see myself working there once I'd finished college. Mike said to give him a call if I wanted a job and Bob gave me a ride across the length of the canteen on top of a wheeled flour bin as a sort of celebration for a successful week. I didn't see Lance to speak to again which suited me as I wouldn't have known what to say ahead of our date. I wondered if Dave had known about the letter, and if so whether he knew that we had agreed to meet. If it had been June and I, she would have known about every stage, she would have advised on the wording of the letter, but I didn't think blokes were quite as involved in each other's lives as girls.

I got home later to find that the outside caterers had phoned offering a last minute job at a wedding the next day and I accepted as I was in need of the money. I was working at the same station as Maureen and felt like pumping her for more information on Lance. But I wasn't sure how to do it without letting her know that we had a date. I didn't think he would appreciate his aunt knowing his business like that.

When we had a moment to spare though I did ask her if she had seen him recently.

'No, I haven't seen him for some time,' she said. 'I see Marie regularly though. I still think of her as my sister-in-law, you know, even though she hasn't been for years. She reckons he's been up and down a bit recently. She thinks he might have a girlfriend hidden away somewhere.'

177

'You don't know who?'

'No, he won't admit to having one. Marie wants him settled, she's always worried he's going to go off and stay with his dad long-term.'

'Would he do that?'

'He keeps threatening to. His job's hardly anything to keep him here.'

'And where does his dad live?'

'Manchester, still. I don't think he'd want him, he's not the best of men, my brother. But Marie would be devastated if Lance even left. She thinks he needs something to keep him here.'

One of the guests on my table was trying to catch my attention so I had to go off and see what he wanted and didn't manage to find out any more information. Asking Maureen for more details about Lance might have seemed a bit odd; I might have seemed a bit too interested.

The wedding seemed to go well. I thought that the bride looked particularly happy. She couldn't have been much older than me. I wondered if this was the happiest day of her life that we girls were always supposed to dream about. I'd seen enough films and read enough books where everything ended happily with a wedding but somehow I'd never imagined it much for myself. I didn't aspire to the wedding and I wasn't desperate to have children which did make me wonder if I was a bit abnormal. It wasn't as if I had high hopes for a great career or anything either. Surely, I thought, I should have something to aim for .

Back at college on Monday I told June about my date that evening.

'Lance?' She sounded surprised. 'What? Lance rather than Dave?'

'Yes, why not Lance rather than Dave? Anyway it is not as if they lined up and invited me to pick one of them. It was Lance who asked.'

'I know, but you shouldn't say yes if he's second best.'

'Why not? You would.'

'Yes, but you're not me, not by a long way.'

'Anyway, he's not second best, not at all. He's got something about him, something you probably haven't seen.'

'Well you're right,' she admitted, 'I don't know him hardly at all. I just had this idea of you and Dave together I suppose. You tell him I'll be after him if he doesn't treat you right though.'

I left college at four, intent on getting home and having a shower and trying to make a bit of an effort with my make-up. On the way home though, going round a tight left-hand bend my scooter hit what I later decided was a patch of diesel spread across the road. The scooter skidded and we parted company. It went left and I went right, hitting the ground face and chest first and continuing the skid on my own. My helmet was open face and my chin hit the road and bounced up making me bite my tongue. Luckily there was no other traffic on the road. I stood up and staggered over to my scooter intent on getting both it and me off the road. There was something loose in my mouth. I spat it out into my hand. It looked like part of a tooth. With my tongue I felt a gap between my front teeth, one of them had chipped off. The gap felt huge.

I picked my scooter up. The side panel was scraped but otherwise it didn't look too bad. I wheeled it off the road and parked it up on the grass verge. I examined myself. Both knees of my jeans and the elbows on my jacket were worn through. I could see the skin through the holes and all of it seemed to be raw with friction burns. My chin seemed to be bleeding and the end of my nose was sore. I was about three miles from home and there was no way I was going to push the scooter that far. I was going to have to see if I could get it to go and get it to go straight.

Feeling very wobbly, it took me three attempts before I was able to kick the pedal with enough force to get it going. The engine sounded pretty normal and so I got on and continued on my way very slowly and carefully, scanning the road ahead of me for any potential hazards.

Mum was in the kitchen when I limped in.

'What happened to you?' she asked.

'I came off my scooter. I need to look in the mirror.' I croaked in answer. My tongue had been exploring the broken tooth the whole way home. I was certain the gap was big enough to fit a straw through. I examined my reflection. My whole chin was red and scraped as was the tip of my nose. The broken tooth didn't look as bad as I had imagined it but it was clearly broken.

'I look as though I've been in a fight,' I said miserably to Mum.

'A fight with an unrelenting piece of tarmac, by the looks of things,' she replied. She had a dishcloth in her hand and was advancing with it in a way that suggested she was going to attempt to clean my grazes with it. I held my arms in front of my face to protect it and she saw the damage to my jacket.

'Oh, what have you done to yourself?' she exclaimed. 'You need to wash all this grit out before it dries in the cuts.' She hustled me upstairs and into the shower where she stood ready to help.

'Go away, Mum. I can clean them myself.' I pushed her out.

I turned the shower to as hot as I could stand it and stood in there for ages concentrating on the water cascading onto my head and down my back rather than on any specific cleaning operations. I got out and wrapped myself in a towel and went and lay down on my bed. It was ages before I could rouse myself. I remembered that Lance was supposed to be coming round and finally made an effort to move.

Clothing was a problem as I didn't want anything near the grazes. I settled on a plain skirt that ended above the knees and a short sleeved t shirt. I dried my hair and lined my eyes with eyeliner and mascara. I went downstairs.

Mum took one look at me.

'You're not going out, after that accident are you?' she asked.

'Yes. I'm not phoning him up and telling him not to come. He'll probably never ask again.'

'If he's any sort of boy you want to spend time with, I am sure he will,' she argued.

I shrugged. 'Well I'm not phoning.'

'Do you want me to?'

'No!'

I sat down carefully, the blood was beginning to dry and movement was becoming a little difficult. I didn't fancy any tea and sat there wordlessly in the kitchen as both Dad and Julia came in and made their comments. I just looked at them mournfully.

I wasn't really in the mood for Lance coming round and by 8pm I could happily have gone to bed. The kitchen window was open and I heard the unmistakable sound of his scooter as he came down the road and into the cul-de-sac. I went out to meet him.

'What happened to you?' he asked as he was taking his helmet off.

'I came off my scooter.'

'Oh. Is it okay? Sorry,' he stopped himself, 'I meant are you okay?'

'Sort of. I broke a tooth.' I was trying to keep my upper lip over my teeth to hide it but I thought I might as well be up front about it.

'And grazed your face and your knees,' Lance added. He looked like he wanted to give me a hug but I was stood with my arms hugging myself so there was nowhere for him to get in.

'Yes.' I nodded miserably.

'Do you want to go out?' he asked, 'or leave it for another time.'

'Leave it for another time, I think,' I answered.

'Okay. How's the scooter, though?'

'I don't know really. I rode it home.'

'Do you want me to have a look at it?'

'Yes, would you?'

I took Lance through to the garden, where I had parked the scooter. He looked like he had made an effort with his clothes; he seemed to have some kind of suit trousers on and a white shirt under his jacket. I didn't want him getting them oily. He didn't seem to be too concerned though and immediately crouched down to look the scooter over. In a couple of minutes he had it practically upside down.

'I think it needs a bit of work, you know,' he said. 'I've got some tools on my scoot, I could do it for you now.'

'If you don't mind,' I said. 'Would you like a coffee?'

He said he would and I went inside to make him a drink. The kitchen door was closed and I heard Mum and Dad talking.

'I'm worried about her,' Mum was saying, 'What if something worse happens to her and I'm not here.'

'Well you could just stop her from using that scooter,' Dad replied.

'I suppose, but if it's not that, it'll be something else. I don't know, you think seventeen's grown up and it just isn't.'

'She thinks seventeen is grown up, that's the problem,' said Dad.

I opened the door and they stopped talking.

'Everything alright?' Mum asked brightly.

I nodded. 'We're not going out. Lance is looking at my scooter for me.'

'He's useful then. Bring him in for a bit of cake when he's done if you like.'

I made us both coffees and took them out to the garden. I sat on the doorstep while Lance took my scooter apart. It was a sunny evening and I was quite happy sitting there watching him work. He was trying to explain what he was doing as he worked. I tried to sound as if I understood but once it got past brakes and spark plugs I was lost.

After a while, Dad came out and he was a much better audience for Lance. He asked the right questions and wandered off to the garage to get extra tools. At one point my scooter seemed to have been broken down into its component parts but after a while, the two of them began to put it back together. When it was back in one piece, Lance asked if he could take it round the block to test it out.

When he had gone, Dad said: 'Nice bloke, you've got there.'

'He's not mine, Dad.'

'Not yet, perhaps, but I think you could work on him. He's not going to spend an evening fixing your scooter if he doesn't like you.' He went back inside.

I waited for Lance to reappear. He did so weaving from side to side across the road, just because he could, presumably.

He parked up next to me.

'There, I think that's fixed it,' he said. 'Bring it up to mine sometime and I'll sort out the bodywork for you.' He seemed to have forgotten that we were supposed to have been on a date. It was as though I was a mate that he was helping out.

I walked over to his scooter.

'How is yours going?' I asked.

'Pretty good,' he answered. 'I still have it broken down more often than it's in one piece, but that's because I can't help tinkering with it. We've done Torquay and Yarmouth together this season and should make it up to Newark on Friday. Are you going?'

'I don't know. The Sessex Girls are going, but I haven't decided yet. I was thinking maybe yes, but after today, I'm thinking maybe no.'

'You shouldn't let little accidents like that put you off. You have to get back on the road as soon as you can.'

'Yes, I'm sure you're right.'

I took Lance inside to wash his hands and, after refusing Mum's offer of a slice of fruit cake, he made to leave.

'Look, we'll try this again, shall we?' he asked as he put on his helmet, 'next week or something?'

'Yes, after Newark.' I was pushing him, but he wasn't going to rise to it, he wasn't going to invite me to go with him or arrange to meet me there.

'Okay, do you want to say a day now, or leave it and I'll give you a ring after the weekend?'

'Give me a ring, do you have my number?'

185

He didn't so I wrote it down for him and he stuffed it in his pocket and said goodbye. There was no kiss this time.

I spent most of the next day in bed, embarrassed and depressed about the accident and how I looked. On Wednesday I managed to drag myself into college although I did go by bus.

June was aghast at the look of me. I told her I was fine as I didn't really want to talk about it, or my evening with Lance. I tried to keep my head down in classes but it was clear to anyone from a brief glance that I had had some sort of accident.

'Nasty carpet burns, you've got there,' said Steve. I ignored him. Some of the others were more sympathetic.

'I'm not going to Newark,' I told June at lunch.

'Good,' she replied. 'Well, I don't mean that, well I do mean that but only selfishly. It's only that Ben's mum says it's okay for him to have visitors so I thought I might go up on Saturday and I was hoping you would come with me.'

I agreed that I would. At least it would mean that I wouldn't be sitting at home moping.

Chapter Fifteen

I was nervous about what we would find at the hospital on Saturday. I knew Ben had to be getting better because he was allowed visitors but I was still worried that he would be changed in some way.

I needn't have worried. He seemed almost back to his usual self, apart from the missing hair and the visible scars. He had been moved into a regular ward and had on some old man's stripy pyjamas. June made some comment about them.

'Yeah well, my mum had to go out and buy them specially. I don't normally wear any.'

He seemed more concerned about me since my grazes were very obvious. I kept catching the rough edge of the broken tooth and had added a torn lip to my list of injuries. He wanted to know what he had missed out on. He didn't have any memory of Yarmouth at all. I didn't remind him that he was supposed to have been meeting me, I just kept it to a description of the all-dayer and being asked to join the Sessex Girls.

'And she's been on a date with Lance,' added June.

'I haven't. It was the day of my accident and he just fixed my scooter,' I said.

I wanted to underplay the idea that Lance had actually asked me out, I wasn't sure what Ben's reaction would be to have all these changes happening while he was comatose.

'I tried to get the doctors to let me out for Newark,' he said, 'but they weren't having any.'

'So when do you think you'll be out?' I asked.

'A couple of weeks, hopefully,' he said. 'Tom says he's got my scooter in a garage and its being fixed up. I reckon I might be on the road in time for Isle of Wight.'

'Aren't you scared?' I asked.

'Of getting back on it? No. I don't remember coming off it so I've nothing to be scared of,' he said. 'I'm not going to drink and ride again though.'

'Good,' said June and I together.

We'd brought Ben a few presents, mainly chocolates and biscuits so we sat and ate those and then left. His mum had left us to it, but on the way out she commented on the grazes on my face.

'That wasn't a scooter accident was it?'

I wanted to lie, but I couldn't think of another way that I might have received such injuries quickly enough so I told her that it was.

'Oh, I really think they should be banned,' she said angrily. I thought that Ben might have more trouble getting back on his scooter again than he had anticipated.

Late on Saturday night the phone rang. No one usually ever phoned past nine so it was a bit of a shock. I was the only person still up and I stood looking at the phone for several rings deciding whether I should answer it or not.

Eventually, when it became clear that whoever was at the other end really wanted someone at my end to pick up, I picked up.

'Hello,' said the person at the other end, 'is that Annie?'

'Yes, it is,' I answered.

'Oh, hello, it's Salty, I mean Lance.'

'Oh, are you okay? You're not broken down anywhere are you?'

'No, no. I'm here at Newark. I just found your number in my pocket and I decided to give you a ring, is that okay?' He sounded either really happy or quite drunk.

'It's okay, but it's quite late,' I said. Mum appeared at the top of the stairs. I looked up and gestured that it was my phone call and she wandered back off again. I sat down on the bottom stair.

'I was phoning to see if you were here or not,' he said.

'And since I answered . . .'

'You're not,' he finished for me. 'Oh well, saves me having to look for you.'

'Why did you . . . want me?' I asked.

'Well you know, there's thousands of people here, I'm with my mates, the music's good, the beer's cheap. But all of a sudden I wished you were here.'

I didn't know what to say.

'Don't suppose you can get here can you?' he asked.

189

'I don't think so.'

'No. Silly question really.'

The pips went and I heard him feed in more money. I wasn't sure why as I didn't know what else there was to say. Then I thought that I was fed up with not getting anywhere so I said: 'Look if you want to you can come round here tomorrow on the way home.'

'I don't think your house is on the way home from Newark,' he said. So he wasn't that drunk.

'No. No, you're right. It was just a thought.'

'Well, I don't know, I might. Don't wait in especially though.'

'Okay, well maybe I'll see you tomorrow then?'

'Yup. Okay.' He hung up.

I hung up too but sat on the stairs for quite a while longer. I wondered what he was doing and whether he would come round. I wondered whether I wanted him to. Drunken phone calls at 11pm before we were even going out with each other weren't a good sign I didn't think.

Sunday came and I did make an effort with my clothes, just in case Lance did show up. My face was looking better, I was left with just the graze on my chin which was still sore but not overly visible from the front.

It was a nice day and I spent it sat outside in the garden reading a book. Mum came out to join me for a bit.

'How are you getting on with your plans?' I asked her.

'My plans?'

'Yes, you know for working your way round the world.'

'Oh, nowhere. Dad and I thought that perhaps it wasn't such a good idea after all.'

'Because of me?'

'You heard our conversation the other day?' I nodded.

'Well, yes, in part because of you, but it was always something I dreamed of, not something I was ever actually going to have.'

'Why not?'

'Because things like that don't come to people like me.'

'What do you mean by that?'

'Well I'm not the right sort. I've got no qualifications for a start, no experience, no knowledge of any other languages. I don't have anything that anyone else would want. Apart from being a Mum to you and Julia and looking after Dad, I'm largely useless.'

'Oh Mum.'

She shrugged. 'You know I'd probably have been away for a week and wanted to come home again. I'm just a bit lost right now that's all and travelling seemed glamorous and exciting. Every woman wants glamour and excitement at some point in her life, even you will some day.

'I want excitement, right now.'

'Yes, you're not looking for glamour though are you?' she said looking pointedly at my clothes.

'I didn't think you were. Weren't you looking to volunteer? Anyway I've made an effort today,' I said.

'You've put a skirt on you mean.'

'Well you know I don't go for all that girly stuff. You've got Julia for that.'

'Yes. Now I have set her off, you know. She's applied to become a children's rep with a holiday company.'

'Really?'

'Yes, she's got an interview next week. Apparently the season's already started but if they like her, they'll put her on a waiting list and then if anything comes up they'll give her a ring and she'll have to be ready to fly out.'

'Wow,' I said, surprised. 'What does Barry think of this?'

'I don't know. I'm not sure she's told him. She didn't tell me until this morning.'

'And where would she go?'

'Somewhere on the Med, probably.'

'Oh well, at least you'll be able to go and visit her if it comes off.'

'Yes. Maybe we could all have a trip. I miss spending time with you. It's like we just pass each other in the kitchen these days.'

'Are you lonely, Mum?'

She looked close to tears. 'Yes, sometimes I am.'

'We need to find you something new to do then, don't we?' I said.

'It's not your problem Annie.'

'No but I could help, couldn't I? Be useful for once?'

'Maybe. We'll see.'

In the evening, I sat out on the front doorstep with my book. I wasn't reading it though, I was listening out for the sound of a scooter above the sounds of children playing in their gardens. There wasn't much traffic that went down our road anyway so anytime there was any engine noise, I listened harder only to be disappointed when it got closer and I realised that it didn't have that distinctive scooter sound.

Slowly the evening turned into night and the children's voices quietened. Eventually I went inside. I knew he wasn't coming. I thought he might have phoned and briefly considered phoning him but decided against it.

Monday and Tuesday evenings progressed in a similar way, even though I wasn't really expecting him anymore. I had thought he was going to phone to arrange another date but perhaps he had forgotten about that, or worse, changed his mind. June wasn't much help. She clearly didn't rate Lance and kept on trying to persuade me to give Dave a ring instead.

'I don't have his number,' I told her.

'I do.'

'How did you get his number?' I asked.

'Best you don't know,' she replied. 'But take it anyway.'

I refused. I was resigned to playing this waiting game with Lance. I would see him sooner or later.

Although we still had a few weeks to go, college was starting to wind down for the summer. June and I took to wandering off to the bank of the river that cut through the town centre at lunchtime and sometimes we forgot to return for afternoon classes.

'They'll only be revising what we've learnt already,' she reasoned. She said she needed the break as she had got herself four weeks' summer work at Debenhams.

'They were begging me to come back,' she boasted.

'I'm not surprised, what must the staff turnover be like there?' I asked.

'Don't be snooty about it, it's easy money,' she told me.

I hadn't got any summer work. Mike had told me to give him a ring if I wanted any, but I was nervous of going back up to Crendell's. I was hoping Julia would get the call from the holiday company and I wanted to have free time in case we got to go out and visit her.

When I got home on the Friday, it looked as though my wishes had been realised as Julia was full of the news that she had been found a position in Ibiza and was due to fly out a week on Tuesday.

'I have to go to London next week and get my uniform and do two day's training,' she told me.

'Two day's training and then they let you loose with a gang of kids?' I asked.

'There'll be a whole team of us,' she assured me.

'And what about Barry?'

'We're going to see where we are after the summer. I'll be back in October, that's only four months. He'll cope.'

I was certain he would cope, but I thought he might be finding other girls to do his coping with.

Mum was very excited for Julia. It was almost as if she were going herself.

'We'll wait to find out where Julia's based and then we'll see if we can book ourselves in for a week in August,' she told me.

The promise of a trip to somewhere warm with a beach cheered me up no end. I had never even been on a plane so that was going to be exciting in itself.

'Not Bank Holiday week, though Mum,' I told her, 'that's the Isle of Wight rally.'

'You're not going all that way on a scooter are you?'

I shrugged. 'Maybe.' I didn't know that I was but I wanted to keep my options open. I thought the girls would be going at the very least.

Chapter Sixteen

I had arranged to meet the girls at the Red Cow on the Wednesday evening. I still felt like a very junior member, especially as they had all been to Newark together since I had joined, but they were always very friendly to me. This time I had persuaded June to come along as well.

I got there early, hoping to get in the car park before Lance so that if he came he would have to come over and see me, rather than the other way on.

I parked up and waited to see who would arrive next. Luckily June arrived soon after. She was itching for a word with Lance even though I had asked her not to.

'I want to tell him to sort himself out,' she said. 'If he wants you he should tell you straight out.'

'Perhaps, but I don't think you telling him that is going to help anything. You'll put him off completely.'

'Well shall I tell Dave you really, really like him instead? That'll make Salty buck his ideas up.'

'No. Thank you. Your efforts to help are not appreciated. Keep your nose out.' I squashed the end of her nose with my finger as I said this and a mock fight ensued. It felt good to have June around. She stopped me thinking too hard about myself.

'Look shall we go in?' I said. I didn't want to be watching every scooter that arrived to see if one of them was Lance.

There were only about half a dozen people in the room when we went in. June headed straight over to the DJ and requested a song. When it came on she dragged me on to the floor and began to dance. I felt a bit self-conscious but danced with her anyway. Pretty soon the room began to fill up and we were no longer alone on the dance floor or the centre of attention.

Andrea and Sarah came over and danced with us. I introduced June to them but over the music it was quite impossible to have a conversation and everyone just nodded to each other. After a while I came off the dance floor and went over to say hello to Sam and Suzy who were over in a corner near the bar.

'How was Newark?' I asked.

'In the middle of nowhere,' said Suzy.

'It didn't matter though,' said Sam. We just stayed on site.'

'Yeah, we didn't see much of you did we?' Suzy said to Sam.

She shrugged, grinning.

'She got back with Dave,' Suzy explained to me.

'Oh. Wow,' I said. 'Congratulations. You sorted out all your issues then?'

'Yeah. We kind of did a bit of growing up while we were apart I think. We did talk about you a bit, I hope you don't mind.'

'I don't know, it depends what you said about me.'

'Oh, well nothing nasty. Mainly about why he asked you to the football.'

'And why did he?'

'Well, I hope this won't sound mean, because it's not supposed to, but he said it was because you reminded him of me.'

'Oh.' That didn't sound mean, but it did hurt. So he hadn't asked me out for me, but because I reminded him of someone else. And presumably I didn't match up because he didn't ask me out again.

'I'm sorry,' said Sam. 'That wasn't a nice thing to say, was it?' My disappointment must have been obvious on my face.

'I don't know,' I said. 'It's not that I don't want to be compared to you, it's the fact that I fell short. It makes me only half a person somehow.'

'I don't think you should read it like that,' said Sam, 'there's much more to it. It's not just about whether you measure up to me or not.'

'No,' said Suzy, 'You know, Dave no doubt realised that it wasn't a right thing to do. You can't replace someone with someone else just because they look like the first person.'

'I suppose.'

'Also,' said Sam, 'I don't know that I should be saying this really, because it's not my place to, but there's the whole thing with Salty too.'

'What whole thing?'

'Don't you know?'

'I don't know whether I know or not.'

'Oh well then, you probably don't, so maybe I shouldn't be telling you.'

'I think you'll have to now you've suggested that there's something to tell,' said Suzy.

Sam looked around the room, presumably to see if Lance or Dave were anywhere around. I had a quick look myself, I couldn't see them.

'Okay. Well what do you know about Lance's family?'

'Bits and pieces, I said, 'I know his dad is up in Manchester somewhere.'

'Okay. Did you also know that he has a two half-sisters?'

I sort of nodded, although I hadn't known this.

'Well, probably about three years ago, he and Dave went up there for a visit. I think they'd both just passed their motorbike tests or something. Anyway, I don't know exactly what happened, but Dave got a bit too friendly with one of Salty's sisters. She was only fourteen or fifteen at the time and when Salty found out he was really angry.'

'Yeah, really angry,' added Suzy. 'I remember that time, everyone avoided him because he was likely to go off on the smallest thing. And then he wrote off his scooter, which just made him more angry.'

'And it wasn't just the fact that his sister was too young, 'said Sam, 'it was the fact that Dave was making himself popular with his family. His

199

dad didn't mind that Dave had shagged his daughter and he supposedly treated him like a long lost son or something.'

'Oh,' I said. 'But how does that relate to Dave and I going out, or not going out?'

'Well, that's a bit complicated, I suppose' said Sam. 'What we've just told you is common knowledge so you could have picked it up anywhere, but this is a bit more personal to Salty.'

'So you shouldn't be telling me?'

'Not really. However . . .' Sam seemed to be trying to think of some way to get her thoughts out right.

'Go on,' I urged her. I needed to know what whatever it was now. 'I'll come to my own conclusions if you don't tell me.'

'Well, I suppose there's the whole thing about Dave not getting close to anyone that Lance wants to be close to. But it's not quite that simple.'

'Oh, why not?'

Sam looked around again to check that no one was listening. 'Well, you remind both of them of his sister.'

'Oh.' I seemed to have my mouth permanently in a circle ready to utter an 'oh' after each new revelation. 'How come I just remind them of other people?'

'Well I don't think it's down to looks in this case. You must be about the same age for a start and Stacey's just got herself a scooter too, her dad bought it for her.'

'Oh. It sounds as though I should just steer clear of all of them.' I said eventually.

Suzy nodded. 'Probably.'

'How come neither of them told me about all this though?' I asked.

'Well, it's obvious isn't it,' said Sam, 'they're blokes, they don't talk about anything important. Most of Salty's anger was a result of the fact that he and Dave didn't talk about what they both thought about it all. Dave thought it was just because she was young, he didn't get the whole family thing for ages.'

'Yes, and the only reason, we know all about it now is because Sam asked the right questions,' added Suzy.

'So are you meeting Dave here tonight?' I asked Sam.

'Yes, he'll be here soon.'

'I might go then, I'm not sure I want to see either him or Lance right now.' I got up to leave.

'Yeah, well, give us a ring if you want to talk about anything,' said Sam.

I nodded. 'Thanks.'

'Oh, while I remember,' Sam said, 'Isle of Wight. We've kind of agreed to all go together, us and the SeaDogs. Part of my new understanding with Dave. So I'm booking the ferry. Do you want to come?'

'Oh. Well I do, but you've just given me a lot to think about. Can I let you know?'

'Okay,' Sam replied, 'but don't leave it too long.

I went over and told June I was leaving. She looked surprised.

'I've just found out some stuff,' I told her, 'I'll tell you about it tomorrow.'

She nodded. 'Okay. I'm not going, I'm having too much fun.' She and Andrea seemed to be getting on very well, so I left them to it.

I got down the steps and out of the door safely, but then noticed both Lance and Dave crossing the road from the car park. I didn't really want to speak to either of them so I pretended not to have noticed them and to be concentrating on looking to see whether it was safe to cross the road. It was, so I began to cross, just as they reached my side.

'Hi Annie,' one of them said.

I looked up, pretending to have noticed them for the first time. 'Oh, hi.'

'Are you going already?' Dave asked.

'Yes, I've got something on tomorrow. See you.' I carried on to the car park.

I saw one of them turn and follow me. I busied myself with looking for my key.

'Annie.' It was Lance 'Look sorry I didn't come round after Newark.'

I shrugged. 'Doesn't matter. I didn't wait in especially.'

'No, well. I thought you might have thought that phone call was a bit odd. I was a bit embarrassed after. I didn't realise it was so late. Or that I was so drunk.'

I shrugged again.

'Look,' he said, 'there's something important I want to say. I'm going away for a bit. Going to see my dad, after Dunbar.'

202

'Dunbar?'

'Yes. Scooter rally. Couple of weeks. Anyway, I do want to see you. But I want it to be right. So I wondered if you would come away with me for a night, this weekend?'

'A night?' I said this to myself, trying to make sense of what he was asking.

'Yes.' He had a hopeful kind of look about him.

'Well, I don't know. It's a bit sudden and there's a lot of stuff going on. Can I have a think about it?'

He nodded.

'Give me a ring, tomorrow evening,' I said. 'I'll let you know then.'

'Okay.'

'Lance, ' I said as he turned to go. 'Thank you for asking.'

He smiled at me. 'I can't fault you for politeness,' he said, as if he could fault me for all kinds of other things.

I rode home slowly. I was trying to make sense of it all. So both Lance and Dave thought I reminded them of Lance's sister, who Dave had slept with three years ago and upset Lance in the process. Dave had asked me out because I reminded him of Sam, who he split up with but then, presumably realised that it was not a good idea and didn't ask me again.

I was okay with Dave's position I thought. But I wasn't so sure about Lance's. Reminding him of his sister might explain some of his protective impulses but what about the hand-holding and the kiss? Should I now think of them in brotherly-sisterly terms rather than sexual ones? It was all very confusing.

But if the thought of me as a sister, why was he asking me away for a night? I wondered what my parents would say if I told them I was going away with Lance.

That thought gave me an idea. Perhaps I would tell Mum that Lance had asked to take me away for a night and decide what to do based on her response.

I rode home in a more relaxed state because I felt that the decision had been taken out of my hands.

When I got home, both Mum and Dad were sat watching the television. I decided to ask them both.

'Mum,' I said, 'Lance has asked if I would like to stay a night away with him this weekend. I haven't said yes or no yet. Do you think it is a good idea?'

She looked almost shocked to be asked. Perhaps I hadn't involved her very much in any of my decisions recently.

'Well I don't know, Annie. What do you think, Jim?

'He seems a decent chap. I'm not sure you're ready for a night away with him though.'

'Dad, I've been away for the weekend twice in the past few months and neither time did you know who I was with or whether they were decent.'

'So you're not really looking for our permission then?'

'I don't know. I suppose I wanted you to be either totally positive about it or totally negative and then either way I'd know what to do.'

'And either way, you'd have chosen to say yes to him, since that's what you really want to do anyway,' said Mum.

As she said that, I knew what she said to be true. I did want to say yes. My instinct was to find out more about Lance, not to close down the possibility that we might have something.

'So what will you say if I say that I'm going?' I asked.

'Is there any point in us saying anything?' Dad said.

'No, not really.'

'Well go then,' said Dad. 'You know, your Mum and I have spent seventeen years trying to teach you what's right and wrong. If you don't know now, you never will and there's nothing we can do about it.'

'So you think it's the wrong idea then?'

'Not necessarily, no. I am just hoping that you will know if it starts to go wrong and will know how to get out of it if it does,' he said.

'Thanks, Dad.' I got up and gave him a kiss on his forehead.

'What for?'

'The vote of confidence.'

Chapter Seventeen

Having made my decision, I was ready to tell Lance straight away. I thought it might look a bit too keen though, so I waited for him to phone the following evening.

I told June the edited highlights of my conversation with Sam at college in the morning. She brushed aside all the issues about Lance mixing me up with his sister.

'Psychological mumbo-jumbo,' she said. 'Look he's asked you to go away with him. He wouldn't do that if he was confused about you, would he? Say yes, go away, get it all over and done with. If you never see him again, at least you'll have lost your cherry.'

I couldn't argue with that. The age of eighteen was approaching fast and I didn't want to still have to admit to being a virgin two years after I had legally been allowed to do it. Although that was not my over-riding reason for going, I told myself.

'That Andrea's nice, isn't she?' June said.

'Yes,' I answered. 'You know she's a lesbian, don't you?'

'No! I like her even more now,' June replied happily.

Lance phoned at 7pm that evening. He sounded nervous. He made sure it was me he was talking to and introduced himself but he left it up to me to bring up the subject of why he was calling.

'Yes please,' I said, 'I would like to go away with you.' I nearly said 'run away with you'. It did feel a bit as if that was what we were doing, even if I did have my parents' sort-of permission.

'Good,' he said. 'I'll pick you up at three on Saturday then. In the car.'

'Okay,' I replied. 'Where are we going?'

'Clacton.'

'Oh. Okay.' I could think of more romantic places.

I spent most of Friday night and Saturday morning wondering what to pack. I didn't really have any suitable clothes for if we were going to stay in a hotel. I thought about asking Julia if I could borrow any of her clothes, but she seemed to have packed all of them already. In the end I settled for a couple of skirts and a pair of jeans for if it was chilly and a few plain tops. I also put in the boating jacket I had made when I was into being a Mod. Boating jackets didn't come in girls' sizes so I had adapted a plain blazer pattern and made it out of a striped woollen fabric.

I was ready to go by ten o'clock and paced around the kitchen until I annoyed Mum to the extent that she allowed me to go and watch television.

Lance was ten minutes late. I went to the loo three times in the half hour before he showed up and when I heard his car pull up, went in the bathroom again.

'Not nervous are you?' asked Julia who was hanging around to get a glimpse of Lance, having missed him on the times he had come round before.

'No. Just making sure I don't need to go on the journey.'

'You'll be back in time for dinner on Sunday, won't you?' Mum called from the kitchen. She had planned a special going-away dinner for Julia so I had to be back for that.

'Yes, I'll probably be back way before then.'

'Okay, Annie, well take care then. Be sensible.'

'I will Mum.' I walked out to the car. Lance was waiting for me by the passenger door. He opened it for me and took my bag.

He had the same clothes on that he'd had on the night he had ended up fixing my scooter. I could see a small oily patch just below his trouser pocket. Everything looked washed and ironed though and he had clearly tried to do something with his hair, probably involving gel. That was the trouble, I thought, if you wore a crash helmet every day, there was no point in trying to have a hair-do because it would only get messed up anyway, so on those odd days when your head remained uncovered, you didn't know what to do with it with your hair.

Lance got back into the car and we set off. I looked back to see both Mum and Julia staring out of the kitchen window. I managed a brief wave and they waved enthusiastically back.

'I didn't know you had a sister,' he said.

I wanted to say that I hadn't known that he had one either, but thought maybe I'd try and work the conversation round to that subject with a little more subtlety. So, instead I told him about Julia and her new job.

'So we're hoping to go and visit her next month,' I said.

'I've never been abroad,' Lance told me. 'Unless you count the Isle of Wight. That's not abroad, is it?'

'I don't think so. Where did you go when you were young?'

'Nowhere much. Mum and I did day-trips to London and stuff and then I usually had a week or so with my dad up north.'

'Oh. And that's where you're going next week?'

'Yes. Not for a holiday this time, though. He reckons there's a job for me up there, a driving job. A step up from the fork-lifts.'

'So you're going for good?' I felt my stomach drop at the thought.

'I don't know.'

'But what about . .your Mum.' I wanted to say me, what about me?

'She'll be better off without me.'

'Says who?'

'Says me. I just hold her back, without me she could make something of her life.'

'But you don't have to go all the way up north do you? Can't you share a flat or something down here?'

209

He looked at me as though that was something he had not thought of. 'What about all the people who are going to miss you down here? What's going to be left of the SeaDogs if you go?'

'They've already decided. They're renaming themselves the Saltyless SeaDogs. Instead of the S.S.C., it'll be the S.S.S.C.'

'I see.'

'I'll still be a member. I'll still see them on rallies. Up North's where it's at to be a scooterist anyway. We haven't got a clue down south.'

It all seemed so simple.

I wanted to ask what taking me away was all about, but I didn't have the nerve.

We arrived in Clacton and parked on the front. It being a Saturday in July, the place was full of daytrippers. It was all bare skin, ice cream and high spirits. Lance seemed nervous now we had reached our destination.

'I booked us into a hotel on the front,' he said. 'There's nothing really smart here so I expect it'll be full of coach parties.'

We walked along until we found the Hotel Splendide. It looked pretty battered, presumably from the east coast winds, but it had large windows opening onto flower beds and big cane chairs for guests to sit in and admire the view.

We managed the checking in process without too much embarrassment and made our way up to the room. We had a sea view and one bed. I had expected this of course but still, standing there looking at it made me anxious. I didn't know Lance well enough. I needed him to touch me, gently, the way he had done in the past to let me know that this was all going to be okay. I went over to look out of the window. There was a gang of girls walking past, giggling and joking with each other. I wished I was with them, doing childish things, rather than up in the hotel room, getting ready to do a very adult thing.

Lance put the bags down and came over and stood with me.

'We don't have to do anything you know,' he said.

'Isn't that what you brought me here for?'

'Well . . .' He put a hand on my shoulder, 'it has to be right.'

'I know.'

I covered his hand with mine to let him know that it would be.

'Look,' he said, 'it's still early, shall we go and get an ice cream?'

We walked down to the front and bought ice creams from a stall next to the pier, then sat down on the sea wall to eat them. I demolished mine in no time while Lance licked his slowly and carefully. We watched a dad build a sandcastle for his kids. After a while they lost interest and ran off to the sea for a paddle, but he carried on digging furiously as if it was his personal goal to build the biggest sandcastle ever.

'So,' I said, I don't even know where Dunbar is.'

'East of Edinburgh,' he replied. 'About twice as far from here as Manchester.'

'Wow, and you're going all that way by scooter?' I asked.

'Yes, over two days though, we're going Thursday.'

'We?'

'Yes, me and Perry. Not Dave, he's too much of a wimp, can't handle the pace.'

'What about your stuff though? How are you getting that up to Manchester?'

'My dad's coming to collect it, would you believe. He hasn't been this far south since the late sixties to my knowledge.'

'So have he and your Mum not seen each other in all that time?'

'No.' he said shortly.

'How's that going to go then?'

'She says she's going to be out.'

'I know this is a bit of a nosy question,' I started, 'but who do you blame? For the break-up I mean?'

'Well,' he thought about it for a bit, 'I was too young to know anything about it at the time. All I remember is there being me and Mum and then, once every summer, Uncle Ian or someone would drive me up and I'd stay with Dad and Sheila for a week or so. They had a baby, and then another one came along later and so I was always on the side-lines somehow. Dad would be out at work or the pub or something and Sheila would get the job of taking care of me. And she wasn't very keen. So I suppose I blamed her. If she hadn't been where she was, when she was, Mum and Dad would never have split up.'

'Where was she? Where did they meet?'

'Here, supposedly. Clacton, Easter 1964. While the rest of the Mods were fighting Rockers on the beach, my dad was shagging Sheila in an alley. All very Quadrophenia.'

'Make love, not war,' I said.

'Perhaps, but not if you've got a wife and baby at home.'

'No, perhaps not.'

'Anyway. I changed my views over recent years. Something happened one year when I went up there. I took Dave and something happened with him and my sister Stacey. It made me realise that it wasn't necessarily the woman's fault. They're painted as these sort of . . . temptresses who men are powerless to resist. But I don't think that's true any longer.'

'So now you blame your dad?'

'Yes. He got away with it all scot-free from me because I was so desperate to have a dad.'

'I don't understand though, if you now blame your dad, why are you going to live with him?'

'Because I told him what I thought about him and so, twenty years later, he's trying to make it up to me.'

'Is that a reason to give up everything you've got down here though?'

He shrugged. 'Sometimes I don't feel as if I've got much down here. You know I never talk to anyone like we're talking now. No one ever asks my thoughts on anything important. Oh, apart from what's wrong with their scooter that is.'

'So, why, . . . sorry, I have to ask this. Why do you want to . . why have you asked me to . . .'

'Why have I asked you to come away with me?' he asked.

'Yes.'

'Well you know that night in Morecambe when I made you sleep in the car?'

'Mmm'

'It was like I was looking after my little sister. Stacey and I have always been wary of each other. I was the interloper into her otherwise perfect family and she was the person who stole my dad's affections. We've never been mates. So it felt good to look after you, like I was resolving that relationship somehow.'

'Okay.'

'So I had these sort of protective feelings for you. But then when you came to work at Crendell's I got to see that you were a person in your own right. A capable person who could walk into a new place of work and be part of it straight away. So then I began to think about you differently.'

Lance had forgotten about his ice cream and the remnants were starting to drip out of the end of the cone. He threw what was left into his mouth in one go.

'Shall we walk?' he said, indicating the path alongside the beach. I nodded. We started walking, weaving our way in between roller skaters, people with dogs and kids on bikes with stabilisers.

'Anyway once I got those feelings they became a bit consuming. You were all I thought of for a couple of days. Then I came round and you'd had that accident and you were back to being vulnerable again, back to being my little sister.'

'What about that time you phoned me from Newark then. What was that all about?'

'Oh, that. That was when I was drunk and Dave had just got back with Sam. And it made me feel a bit useless, really. I've never managed any sort of relationship at all. So I thought I'd give it a try there and then. I knew you weren't at Newark because I asked Sam, but it seemed a good reason for calling. At the time anyway. Not very sensible really.'

'Why not?'

'Because it should be right.'

'This whole thing about it being right, doesn't it hold you back though?'

'Yes. But if it's not right, it's wrong and I couldn't bear for it to be wrong. I don't want to be the one to hurt the other person. I'm trying very hard not to be my dad.'

'But you're not your dad. There's degrees of it being right and wrong, isn't there? And maybe he was really clearly wrong.'

'Okay, but even a little bit wrong can end up being hurtful.'

'Alright,' I said, 'but I still don't know why we're here now. Why haven't you walked away and decided to try elsewhere with someone that you're not so confused about.'

'Because,' he said simply, 'it's still you that I want.'

We had reached the point where the coast changed direction and the sea took over from the land. Few people had walked up this far and for a moment we were all alone. I looked out to the horizon where the grey sea blended into the pale blue of the sky.

'Would it be right if I wanted it too?' I asked.

He nodded. I turned to face him and moved in closer. I put my hand on his shoulder and stretched up to plant a kiss on his mouth. For a moment he didn't react. But then he bent down a little and put both of his hands on my waist. He held me there for a second and then moved his hands to my head where they cupped both of my ears. He kissed me gently and then more strongly and then I began to kiss him back and we were kissing as though there was no one else in the world that mattered.

Chapter Eighteen

We decided to head back into town.

'Shall we walk along the Greensward?' I asked.

'How do you know it's called that?' Lance asked.

'I came to a Radio 1 roadshow here once and that's where they said it was, 'On the Greensward.'

'Was it any good?'

'No, it was rubbish. You're better off listening to it on the radio. Some people are better imagined than seen in the flesh.'

In the town centre we peered in the windows of a few restaurants. There was a Wimpy and a couple of cafes as well as a few smarter restaurants but I couldn't see us being comfortable in any of them.

Lance suggested we go into the one that looked the most expensive. I looked at the menu but the writing was all flowery and overblown.

'You wanted it to be right,' I said, 'and this wouldn't be right.' I told him what I thought might be right. He agreed and we went and bought a bottle of wine from an off-licence and cod and chips from the chippy. We took these to a bench overlooking the sea. Lance had to push the cork into the bottle as we didn't have an opener and we took turns to drink from it.

217

The fish was fresh and the batter was crispy and it was probably one of the best meals I had ever had.

The sun was going down behind the town as we walked back to the hotel. Despite the relaxing effects of the wine, I felt my tension rising. I wondered if the first time was like this for everyone. Perhaps only if it had been planned and anticipated the way ours had. It suddenly occurred to me that this might be Lance's first time too.

'Do you know what to do?' I asked as we climbed the stairs.

'What? Oh. Yes. Enough. Probably.' He tripped on the last step.

Once we were in the room, I went over to the window again. It was dark enough for the street lights to be on and over on the far horizon I could just make out a couple of ship's lights.

Lance came up behind me, put this hands on my shoulders and turned me around to face him.

We looked at and into each other's faces. I noticed that I was holding my arms tightly across my chest and self-consciously let them go loose by my sides.

'Okay?' Lance asked. I nodded. We kissed and he moved his hands slowly down my body until he reached my hips. Then he pulled me in close to him. My senses responded to him and I felt his need. I stood on tiptoe to fit the shape of his body better. We edged toward the bed and fell on to it heavily, side by side.

Lance moved on top of me and worked his hands slowly into a gap between my t-shirt and skirt, finding bare skin and carrying on upwards. I wrapped one of my legs around his.

Suddenly he stopped kissing me.

'I've still got my shoes on,' he said. Getting up from the bed he removed his shoes and socks. Then he rifled around in his bag and took out a small tape player which he put on the bedside table. He pressed 'play' and the sounds of Marvin Gaye filled the room.

'It's probably a bit naff,' he said, 'but I've listened to him for years and I always felt that he was the right accompaniment. Is it okay with you?'

'Yes.'

He turned away and self-consciously took off his trousers. He had on what looked like new white boxers underneath. He was holding a condom packet.

'Should I . . .?' I said, indicating my own clothes.

'I'll help you, shall I?' Lance asked, returning to my side. Together we removed all of our clothing until we were skin to skin.

'You are so beautiful,' he said, running his fingers gently across my curves. We moved together, electrically, magnetically. Everything seemed to fit and my body found new positions to draw him further into me.

When he was done there were beads of sweat across his forehead.

'You didn't . . .?' he asked.

'No.' I had experimented of course, I knew what an orgasm was like. 'But it's okay, really.'

'Maybe next time?' he asked.

'Maybe. Not straight away though?'

'No.' He pulled the bedspread over me and reached for his underwear.

'Don't go,' I said.

He looked at me, confused.

I mean right now. Stay here next to me.'

He lay back down on the bed.

'Was it . . .how you imagined it?' I asked.

He shook his head. 'No, it was very different. Because it was real.'

'Better?'

'Much.'

We lay there for a while, neither of us speaking. The room grew dark and the lights outside shone brighter through the window.

Under the covers Lance explored my body with his fingers. He found places that I kept private from anyone else. Slowly we built the tension until it ran over and my body tensed and then relaxed.

'Thank you,' I whispered.

'No, thank you,' he whispered back. 'It was right. It is right, right now.'

Later still, we decided to go for another walk along the front.

'Do you think they'll lock us out?' I asked

'No, this is a proper hotel, not a B&B, they'll have night porter on.'

We held hands and made jokes about the grumpy faces we could see through hotel lounge windows.

'Does this mean I can call you Salty now?' I asked.

'I suppose. Do you think you will?'

'No. Lance is good enough for me.'

We took our shoes off and went down on the beach. There were a few late dog-walkers around but otherwise we were on our own. Noise from the pier followed us for a bit, but then faded as we climbed over more and more groynes.

'So, what happens now? I asked. 'This time next week, you'll be gone.'

'Yeah. I hadn't thought this far ahead, to be honest.'

'You were concentrating too hard on getting the first time right. Perhaps you didn't think there would be a second?'

'Maybe.'

'Well if you want a fresh start, you'll have to leave me behind too.' Maybe that was what he had planned for. A once-only offer, and a chance to get away scot-free, no opportunity for awkward meetings after the event. He wouldn't have to avoid me, because we wouldn't be in any of the same places. I took my hand out of his on the pretext of pulling my hair out of my eyes and I didn't put it back. I felt lost.

'I will have to leave you behind,' he said. 'There's no getting away from that. I should've been quicker, got together with you earlier then we would have known by now if we had anything. But I can't say whether we have now, it's too soon.'

'So . . .'

'Look,' he said, grabbing for my hand again, 'I'm not going to go up there and forget about this, forget about you. But we'll just have to see.'

We turned and walked back. In the town, the lights in the hotel lounges had mostly gone out. In one, a silhouette of a single man sitting by a bar could be seen. We passed another man with his hood up, having a loud argument with himself.

Back in the room, I showered. I stood under the hot water for a long time. I almost hoped that Lance would be asleep by the time I came out of the bathroom, but he was lying awake, waiting for me.

I climbed in the bed next to him. He pulled me to him and I laid my head on his chest.

'I can't decide,' he said. 'whether to make love to you again and again in the time we've got left, or whether to just hold you.'

'Just hold me, please,' I said.

'Okay.'

After a while his breathing became more steadier and I lay there my head gently rising and falling with his chest. I ran my fingers across his few chest hairs and circled a mole above his left nipple. Eventually in the early hours, I turned away from him and fell asleep hugging a pillow.

Chapter Nineteen

I awoke the next morning to the sound of the bedroom door closing. Lance was standing there with a tray of breakfast things.

'I went down and asked them if I could bring something up,' he said. The sun was shining through the window, highlighting the stubble on his chin. He looked ruffled and tired but also very attractive.

I sat up and he placed the tray in the middle of the bed. Any morning-after-the-night-before awkwardness was masked by concentrating on sorting out the breakfast. There was tea and toast and marmalade and we ate it all in double quick time. I licked the butter and marmalade remnants off my fingers feeling quite cheerful.

'What time do we have to be out of here?' I asked.

'Ten-thirty,' he answered. I looked at the clock, we had an hour and a half.

'Time for a quick one then?'

Lance grinned. He removed the tray and pushed the covers aside. This time I was less reserved. I took the lead and manoeuvred myself astride Lance's hips, controlling the rhythm and concentrating on my own pleasure.

I collapsed on his chest and he held me tight, one hand tangled in my hair.

'Oh God,' was all he could say.

Afterwards we both squeezed into the shower cubicle and soaped each other down. I already felt a familiarity with his body.

'You're making my leaving more difficult,' he said.

'I know,' I replied. 'Don't go then.'

We went for a walk along the pier before we headed back home. We got a pound's worth of two pences and fed them into the waterfall machines, winning back about half of what we put in. Then Lance spent about £3.50 trying to win me a furry dog in the grabber machine. Eventually he successfully caught and held onto a wonky-eyed black dog who we christened Fido.

At the end of the pier we watched the fishermen haul in their lines to see what they had at the end of them. Lance got talking to one of them and asked him questions about the difference between sea fishing and river fishing. As we walked away he said 'That was the one thing Dad and I used to do together.'

'Fishing?'

'Yeah. He had all the kit. But the time I remember most is one time we went to Gill's Meadow. You know, that place we stopped at on the way to Morecambe?'

I nodded.

'Uncle Ian had driven me up and Dad met us there. It was supposed to be some sort of halfway change-over point, although it was much closer to Manchester. Anyway Dad was late and I had thought that he had forgotten but then he showed up with fishing nets and a proper picnic in a wicker basket and we spent the day in the stream trying to catch whatever went past. It was about the only time I remember that there was just the two of us and I had his undivided attention.'

'How old were you?'

'About eight or nine, I think. I'd forgotten about it, but driving up there, the entrance looked familiar and I decided to stop and have a look.'

'And then I disturbed you.'

'Yeah, you came piling in with your big old size fives and spoilt everything.' He gave me a shrug to show that he didn't mean it.

We drove home slowly, Aretha Franklin on the tape player.

'I don't mind a bit of Aretha now and again' said Lance as I sang only badly to '(You Make Me Feel Like) a Natural Woman', 'she seems to fit the mood.

We stopped at a Berni Inn and had steak and strawberries for lunch. I played around with my strawberries, teasing Lance by eating them slowly and suggestively.

When we got back to my village, Lance pulled over before turning into the cul-de-sac.

'I don't really want to be watched by your parents or your sister,' he explained. He moved in closer to me, leaning over the handbrake, and kissed me passionately .

Eventually he moved away and I let out a long breath.

'I go on Thursday,' he said, 'and my dad is coming to pick up my stuff on Wednesday, so can I see you on Tuesday?'

I nodded. 'I think so. I might go with Mum and Dad to take Julia to Gatwick in the morning but I expect we'll be back by the evening.

'Shall I meet you at the Red Cow then? I'll take you up to meet my Mum.'

'Okay.'

I thought of something. 'Are you going to the Isle of Wight?'

'I expect so, but I'll have to see how this new job goes, first. Are you going?'

'I thought I might. Sam said she'd book the ferry for me, She says the girls are going with the SeaDogs.'

'Yeah, that's what I heard too.'

'Do you think it's a bad idea?'

'No. It's not that, it's just that things are changing already and I'm not part of it.'

'Yes. Well. Maybe we'll get to spend the weekend together then, you'll join up with the SeaDogs even if you go down on your own, won't you?'

'Yes. Maybe.'

He started the engine and pulled round the corner and dropped me off, saying goodbye with a quick squeeze of my thigh.

In the kitchen Mum was chopping away at a carrot with a large knife.

'Shall I do that?' I asked. 'I am trained.'

'Go on then,' she said, handing over the knife.

'What are we having?'

'Cheese fondue.'

'How very 1970s.'

' I was casting about for something foreign to make and I found the set in the back of the cupboard.'

'But Julia's going to Spain, not Switzerland.'

'Yes, well, I couldn't think of anything Spanish.'

Paella?' I suggested. 'With a glass of sherry?'

'Isn't sherry from Portugal?'

No, port is from Portugal, I think.'

'Oh.' We were both left pondering on the vastness of our ignorance.

'What's for pudding?' I asked.

'Mandarin cheesecake. That was Julia's choice.'

'Hmm. Cheese followed by cheese.'

'Oh yes,' said Mum, 'I didn't think of that.'

'Oh well,' we both said together, shrugging.

'So how was it?' she asked as I got to work on the vegetables.

'Good, Mum. Really good.'

'Are you seeing him again?'

'Yes, on Tuesday. But then he's going up North.'

'For good?'

'He doesn't know yet.'

227

'Oh, that's a shame. Just your luck to find a nice boy have him leave immediately.'

'I know.' I hadn't sorted out how I felt about it all yet.

The phone rang and I went to answer it. It was June.

'You're back, then,' she said. 'How did it go? What exactly did you do?'

'I'm not telling you exactly what we did!'

'Go on.'

'No, my Mum's in the other room.'

'Okay, well I'll ask the questions and you can just answer yes or no, okay?'

'Yes, okay.'

I answered most of her questions with a yes and a few with a scandalised No! There was much giggling at either end.

'Oh, I forgot to say,' June added, 'Ben should be coming out this week, Tuesday, they think.'

'Is he better?'

'Not really, but he's well enough to be home rather than on the ward. Do you want to come round and see him in the evening.'

'I can't, I'm seeing Lance that evening.'

'Oooh.'

'The last time before he goes.'

'Ahhh. Wednesday or Thursday then?'

'Yes, okay.'

Despite my comments, the fondue was actually quite fun. We got on quite well as a family when we made the effort. Julia was in exceptionally high spirits.

'You should come out for longer than a week,' she told me. 'I'll hide you in my room and you can help me with the kids' club.'

'Thanks.' I would never do it, but I liked the sound of it as an idea. When I reached eighteen, I could apply to do the job myself.

'Freedom, that's what it's all about,' she declared.

'Yes,' said Mum. 'I wish there had been jobs like that around when I was young.'

'Then you'd never have met me,' said Dad. I thought sometimes he wished he'd had a son rather than two girls. He needed another male to bring a bit of balance to the family, someone to talk about cars and football to.

'No, you're right dear and then I'd never have had Julia and Annie and we wouldn't be here talking about this.'

'The road not taken,' said Dad.

'How do you know the right one?' I asked. 'The right road I mean.'

'Well, you don't, do you?' said Julia

'Some you don't get to take because you can't, they're blocked off to you for some reason or another,' added Mum 'and as for the others, you just have to weigh up the pros and cons.'

'Or go with your heart,' said Dad. We all looked at him, surprised that he would come out with such a comment.

'Well, you do,' he shrugged, scraping a bit of celery around the nearly empty fondue dish.

229

'And sometimes you have to take a bit of a leap of faith. I didn't know Mum was going to say yes when I asked her to marry me, but I bought the ring anyway.'

'And here we are, twenty one, long, happy, long years later,' said Mum, giving dad a kiss.

'Urgh,' said Julia and I together, 'keep it to yourselves, can't you?', something we had been saying for years.

'You'll be as old as us, one day,' Dad said, 'and it's only your body that gets old, not your mind, and even your body doesn't forget what makes it happy.'

Chapter Twenty

Monday was the beginning of the last week of college before we broke up for the summer holidays. We really weren't learning anything so I decided to go to Gatwick on Tuesday to see Julia off. I had never been to an airport before so it was all very exciting. I thought of all the people travelling to different countries and of all the different cultures they would encounter.

'Just think,' I said to Julia, 'by teatime, you'll be in Spain.'

'I know,' she replied. Barry hadn't come to see her off. She had asked him and seemed disappointed that he had said no. She thought it was because he was putting his work before her, but I thought it was more likely that he wasn't prepared to watch her leave.

'I have to go through now,' she said, looking at the departure board. We each gave her a hug.

'Phone us as soon as you can and tell us where you are and I'll get straight down the travel agents,' Mum said as Julia queued up to go through the barrier.

She turned and waved and we stood looking at her departing back.

'She'll have changed by the time she comes home,' said Dad. 'Perhaps she won't be our Julia anymore.'

'She'll always be your Julia, Jim,' Mum said, 'even if she does change.'

Our journey back was a bit subdued.

'Just the three of us for tea, then,' said Mum.

'I thought I might just have a sandwich. I'm going to see Lance tonight,' I said.

'Just the two of us, then,' she said to Dad. 'Unless you've got something on?'   Lance was already there when I got to the Red Cow. He was crouched on the ground, the side panel off his scooter, attacking something in the engine with a spanner.

He stood up when he saw me and rubbed his hands on a rag he pulled out of his pocket.

'Is it going to make it? I asked.

'Dunbar? In short stages, maybe.'

'It was your dad's scooter wasn't it? Do you think he'll like it?'

'I dunno.'

'Do you think he'll recognise the meadow?' I asked, pointing to the artwork.

'I don't suppose so.'

'You don't sound too happy.'

'No. Dad says he's not coming down to pick up my stuff after all. I'm going to have to find some other way to get it up there.'

'Oh, sorry.'

He shrugged. 'I have to learn not to rely on him. If I do that and concentrate on sorting myself out, I'll be okay. Anyway, Mum's waiting to meet you, so shall we go?'

Lance led the way, riding slowly so that I could keep up. We headed to an estate north of the town and pulled up outside a small semi that looked the same as all the others along the road.

I parked up next to Lance and took off my helmet.

'Do you think she'll like me?' I whispered as we walked down the side path to the back door.

'Of course. How could she not?' He gave my hand a squeeze.

'What should I call her?'

'Oh. Mrs Morales, probably. Her first name's Marie, though.'

'Marie,' I said, as if I was hearing it for the first time, although I had, of course known her name for months.

She was sat at a small formica table in the kitchen when we went in, smoking a cigarette which she hastily stubbed out when she saw us coming. She closed the magazine she had been reading and stood up to meet me.

'Mum, this is Annie,' Lance said formally. We shook hands.

'Hello Mrs Morales,' I said, 'nice to meet you.'

'You too, darling, call me Marie' she said. 'I'd like to say that Lance has told me a lot about you. But I can't because he hasn't. He don't tell me nothing.' She looked at him pointedly. 'Have a seat, she said to me, 'can I get you a coffee?'

We all sat down around the small table and she made drinks and got out a packet of digestives. Through the back window I could see that the garden was filled with flowers and shrubs of all colours. Mrs Morales asked lots of questions about my parents and what they did and what I was doing at college.

'Make sure you get a qualification,' she told me. 'I always told Lance that, but he ignored me of course. With a qualification you can do a lot more than without one. Look at me.'

'What do you do, Mrs Morales?'

'Marie, please. I work shifts at the Co op down the road and I take in sewing sometimes.'

'Mum does pockets mostly,' added Lance. I looked a bit confused.

'They bring round the trousers and the pocket pieces and I sew them in,' she explained, 'and then they collect them and take them on to the next person who does the zip or whatever.'

'Oh.'

'They pay a few pennies per pocket. It's not going to make me rich.'

'No.' There wasn't much I could say about that. It did sound a bit grim.

'And now I'm losing Lance's rent too.'

'Oh Mum, not now,' he said.

'Oh, it's alright, I'm not going to embarrass you in front of your girlfriend,' she said. My insides jumped at the sound of that word.

'I'm thinking of trading down,' she told me. 'Get a little flat, just room for me. No point in rattling about this big place on my own.'

'But what about your garden?' I asked. 'It looks beautiful, wouldn't you miss it?'

'I would, you know,' she said. 'I could have pots, I suppose, but they're not the same.' She looked mournful.

'I thought I'd take you for a ride,' Lance said quickly. 'On my scooter.'

'Oh. Yes.' I replied. 'We never got to do that.'

I stood up. 'Nice to meet you, Marie,' I said.

'You too,' she said. 'See if you can get Lance to stay, would you?'

'It's not too late to change your mind,' she told him.

'No, Mum,' he said as we walked back outside. It sounded as though she had told him this many times.

'Well, that was my Mum,' he said.

'She's nice,' I said.

'Yeah, she's alright.'

We put our helmets on. 'Where are we going to go?' I asked.

'I haven't decided,' he said. 'We'll see when we get there, shall we? Lance started his scooter up. 'You get on first.'

I climbed on and edged up as far as I could to the back rest. Lance swung his leg over and pushed it off the stand.

'Hold on to my waist,' he directed. I grabbed handfuls of his jacket. 'No, me, not my clothes.' I put my arms around him. We hadn't yet touched and it felt overly intimate as if I had just imagined our night away.

Lance accelerated and we were away. I had to get used to the rhythm of his driving, anticipating the speeding up and the slowing down so I could hold my body right. As we got out of town he sped up and began leaning into the corners and I had to be ready to lean into them with him. After a while, it felt as though we were working together, all three of us, me, Lance and the scooter, as a team. We hit the top of a hill and lifted a little as we broke the crest. I laughed out loud. Lance squeezed my arms underneath his own.

A bit further on he pulled into the entrance to a Common and parked up.
'You're a good passenger,' he said as he got off. 'Want to come to Dunbar?'

'What would you say if I said yes?' I asked.

'Take you, of course. Shall we explore a bit?'

We chose the darkest path and followed it for a while. It opened up at the brow of a hill where open land stretched ahead of us in the dusk, the lights from town, flickering on uncertainly below us.

We sat down among the ferns and dock leaves that made up the majority of the undergrowth in that part of the Common. I watched as another set of street lights came on red and then warmed up to yellow.

'You know Ben's supposed to have come home today?' I said.

'No, I didn't know that.'

'Yes. It's all change this week, Julia's gone, you're going, Ben's coming back. Oh and college finishes on Friday too.'

'So what are you going to do with yourself?'

'Sleep. And hope that when I wake up everything's back to normal.'

'What's normal though? We're not normal. Not yet. We're still at the getting to know each other stage.'

'Yes, why go now? If you leave it another couple of weeks I'll have decided that I don't like you after all and you'll be free to go.'

'Thanks,' he said.

We were sat up close to each other and he had his hand jammed down the back of my jeans where they gaped a little away from my body. Pretty soon he had me down flat on the ground and was covering me with his body, kissing each part of my face in turn.

'Hold on a minute,' I said, pulling on a fern that was tickling my ear. 'I thought you were obsessed with it being right. I'm lying on all sorts of bugs and creepy-crawlies here.

'Oh yeah, sorry. To be honest though, it only has to be right the first time. After that it's every man – or woman – for his or herself.' He did take off his jacket though and spread it out for me to lie on.

'What a gentleman.'

'Thank you.'

After some more kissing and groping, we paused for breath. It was getting too dark to see much.

237

'I suppose we should be getting back soon. I've got to ride home yet,' I said.

'Does that mean I'm not going to get to shag you again?'

'Not unless you are really quick. Anyway maybe it's better, maybe it'll make you want to come back quicker.'

He was on me, fiddling with my trousers and then with his. Anyone passing would have seen writhing bare flesh and heard animal-like grunting. Maybe there were people watching, we did put on a bit of a show.

Later, as we walked back to the scooter, Lance said:

'Well that didn't work.'

'How do you mean?'

'It didn't get you out of my system. I still want you.'

We rode back to his house.

'Well that's it then,' I said. 'So long. Take care.' I didn't want to go, not without some assurance that this wasn't it. I was trying to be brave about it. If I got on my scooter quick, he wouldn't be able to drag this goodbye out for any longer than I could stand.

'You can't go like that,' he said.

'Like what?'

'Like you're not going to let me say goodbye to you properly. Take your helmet off.' I undid the strap and removed it.

He stood close to me and put his arms around my waist. I felt his weight and pressed back against him. We stood like this for some time.

'Maybe you could stay the night?' he asked. I was thinking over whether this was a good idea or not when I heard the noise of an engine and a light shone in my eyes. Two scooters were pulling up in front of the house. Lance and I broke away from each other.

'Sorry mate,' said one of the riders as he got off his scooter, 'I didn't realise you were . . .' he pointed to each of us in turn. I recognised his scooter, it was Perry and one of the other SeaDogs. Bertie, I thought his name was, although I didn't know if that was his real name. He did have a very round face though, which made me wonder if he was named after a liquorice allsort.

'Just wanted to check what the plans were for Dunbar, who's taking what, that sort of thing.' Perry was speaking to Lance but looking me and up and down.

'Hello, he said. I don't think we've had the pleasure.' He held out his hand and I shook it.

'Shall we go inside?' Perry said to Lance.

'I have to go,' I said.

'Oh. Yes.' Lance said. 'Won't be a moment,' he said to Perry who stayed where he was. So we said our goodbyes with an audience.

'You have my number I said. Maybe you could phone. Or write. Letters are good.'

'Yes,' he said. 'I'll do that.' He seemed distracted.

I got on my scooter and kicked the engine over. 'Bye then.'

'Yes. Bye.'

And I rode away.

239

Chapter Twenty One

On Wednesday I managed to make it into college by lunchtime. It was hardly worth it but I had agreed to go with June and see Ben afterwards.

'I thought you weren't coming,' said June when I pitched up in Accommodation Science.

'No, well I wasn't going to, but I did want to see Ben.'

'He'll be pleased to see you,' she said, 'he's a bit bored and desperate for company.

'Have you seen him already then?'

'Yes, I went round last night. I stayed till his mum chucked me out. How about you?' she asked.

'You mean, last night? Yeah, fine. I met his mum, went for a ride on his scooter, said goodbye, came home, end of story.'

'So?'

'So, nothing. He's gone, or going anyway.'

'And what are you going to do?'

'I don't know.'

And I didn't know. Wait for Isle of Wight perhaps, but that was six weeks away.

I followed June's bus back to her village after college and together we went to see Ben. He seemed quite cheerful on the whole.

'It's good to be back in my own room again,' he told me. 'But I'm not supposed to go out

240

much for another few weeks so it looks like I'll have to hole up in here.'

He had a pile of presents from school friends so it looked like he was going to be okay for chocolate.

'No fags though, the doctor said, and no alcohol. No anything really. It's going to be a very boring summer.'

'I'll keep you company,' said June.

'I thought you were working at Debenhams?'

'Yeah, well, when I've finished for the day.'

'What about your scooter?' I asked Ben.

'Well it wasn't waiting for me on the drive when I got home. I think it's still at the garage. I don't think Mum wants me to have it back.'

'Why not?'

'Because she thinks it's not safe. Or she thinks I'm not safe, more likely.'

'What about if you did some training, like Lance suggested?'

'Yeah, maybe.'

'Did you know Annie got it together with Lance?' June asked Ben.

'Yes. You told me yesterday.'

'Oh, yes. So I did. But don't you want to hear all about it from her?'

'Well if she wants to tell me.' Ben said.

'Not really.' I answered. I had had a thought. I needed some sort of focus for the next few weeks, perhaps I could do some training and take my test. I decided to look into it.

241

'You didn't get me a patch did you?' Ben asked.

'From Yarmouth? No.'

'Oh. I didn't get a chance to get one myself.' I nearly said 'Well you should have been more careful then,' but that sounded a bit too much like something his parents might have said to him.

June and I stayed a bit longer and then I went and had tea round at her place. We ate it sat in the sun in her back garden and it was so relaxing, I didn't leave until quite late.

When I got home, Mum as bursting with news.

'Julia phoned. She said she's in a big hotel in Playa d'en Bossa and she's sharing with another rep and it's all going well so far.'

'Mum, she can't have been there 24 hours.'

'No, well, they're the most important hours, you've got to get a good first impression.'

'Anyway,' she continued, 'I went straight down the travel agents and I've got us a week in an apartment down the road from the hotel for the third week in August.'

'Back in time for the Bank Holiday?'

'Yes, three days before, I think. Anyway, the travel agent, Sally, she was ever so nice. I got talking to her about her job and everything. And,' she paused for a moment, 'I think it's something I might do.'

'Be a travel agent?'

'Yes, why not?'

'No reason at all, Mum, I think it's a good idea. Don't you have to have training?'

'Yes, but you can do it on the job, day release at college.'

'Not my college, I hope.'

'Why not?'

'You'd be expecting me to have lunch with you and you'd be checking up on me. You'd really cramp my style.'

'Oh, I don't think so. I can be discreet if I have to be.'

'I don't like to say this Mum, but aren't you too old?'

'Apparently not. There's a whole lot of support for women returners to work, Sally said. I didn't know about any of it.'

'Me either. Oh well, go for it Mum. Do you get to travel so you can tell the customers about the places they want to travel to?'

'Yes, that's the best thing, all the holiday companies are desperate for custom so there's lots of trips. 'Jollies' I think Sally called them.'

'Wow, Mum. Better get your CV together.'

'Yes. I'd better think of something I can put on it first. It's going to be very short otherwise.'

Mum got right on with her CV the next day as well as making sure all our passports were valid and writing a big list of things we needed for our holiday. I felt like she was leaving me behind so I got the telephone book out to see if I could find out about scooter training.

'What are you looking for?' Mum asked.

243

'I need to find a place to do my part one motorbike test.' I told her. I'm going to go for my licence.' Suddenly she looked a bit shifty.

'Oh Annie, I forgot to tell you. Lance phoned yesterday evening. I was supposed to get you to phone back when you got in but I was so full of my own news I forgot.'

'Oh. Mum.'

'Can you ring him now?'

'Not unless he's had a phone installed on his scooter, no. He didn't say anything, did he? Why he was calling?'

'No. He was going to tell you. He said it was okay to phone until quite late, but I just forgot.'

I couldn't think how to fix it. Would he think that I had not phoned on purpose? He hadn't given me his dad's number so I couldn't phone him there. I could call his Mum or Dave and ask them to pass a message on but either option seemed a bit extreme. I was just going to have to wait and see if he phoned again.

I didn't feel like researching motorcycle training after that but the next day I spoke to a motorcyclist in the car park at college and he gave me the name of a school that he had been to. I phoned up and booked myself in for the following week. I was a little bit shocked at the price of it though. My money wasn't going to stretch to that and the Isle of Wight too. There was also Ibiza although I was hoping Mum and Dad would provide spending money for that.

In the end I plucked up courage and phoned Mike at Crendell's. He seemed pleased to hear from me and gave me a week's work at the beginning of August filling in for kitchen porter Bob.

'Saves me having to go to a temp agency and pay their over-inflated rates,' he told me.

So I was beginning to have something of a structure to the summer. June and I celebrated the end of term in usual style in the college bar at lunchtime. Most of June's conversation centred on Ben. She had been to see him again on Thursday evening and was planning on going again after the bar closed that afternoon.

'Haven't you run out of things to talk about yet?' I asked.

'No, his Mum's found some of their old board games, so yesterday we had a game of Chartbusters and today it's Cluedo.'

'Does Tom join you?'

'He hasn't yet. In fact I haven't seen him since Ben came home. He seems to be busy with something, I don't know what.'

'Maybe he's busy with someone?'

'Maybe.'

'And you don't mind?'

'No, why should I? We were only passing time.'

'So when am I going to see you again?' I asked after a while.

'Well you're welcome anytime,' she answered. Try Debenhams, then Ben's then mine.'

'You never come to mine.'

'No. That's because you live in the back of beyond. A person would have to be really committed to actually visit you at your house.'

'Like Lance?'

'Yeah, I think he was keen.'

'Was.' I told her about not returning his phone call.

'You think about things too much, Annie,' June said, 'and everything ends up as a negative. So you missed a phone call, so what? If he had anything important he wanted to say to you he should have said it while you were together. If it's that important he'll try again.'

'I suppose.'

I tell you what, next time you're on your scooter, try shouting all your thoughts about him out. Leave them behind you. Concentrate on looking forward and see what happens next.

I did try, but it didn't stop me hovering by the phone willing it to ring even though I knew Lance would be busy with his scooter rally mates. Dunbar seemed like a world away and somehow I couldn't imagine anyone being able to get through on the phone from that distance.

He didn't phone and he didn't write. I spent most of the following week in the garden when the sun came out and helping Mum put her job application together when it went in.

'You have to make out that being a Mum's like a job,' I told her. 'Say something about your organisational capabilities used to get everyone out of the door in the morning and your persistence in making everyone see your point of view, that kind of thing.'

She actually had quite a lot to write about when she got on to her volunteering as, although it was unpaid, it seemed to have been really useful and important.

'I never knew you did all that, Mum. Those old people rely on you.'

'I did keep asking you to come along and see for yourself, you know,' she replied. 'You're so obsessed with yourself sometimes, Annie, you don't have time to see what everyone else is up to.'

I was beginning to think that perhaps everyone had a point. Perhaps I was too caught up with myself. Perhaps I should be trying to look more outwardly and spend more time on thinking about other people. The only thing I knew about a lot of so-called friends was what they had revealed to me, because I wasn't very good at asking the questions that might make them open up to me. Perhaps I just had to be more nosey.

I decided to practise my new persona out on the other people on my motorcycle training course. It was a whole day affair. We were to start in the morning with slow stuff round bollards in a car park and if we passed those we'd have part one of the test. In the afternoon we were to go out on the road following the instructor who would train us in what was expected for part two.

There were five of us on the course. Predictably all the others were men on motorcycles of one sort or another. A couple looked at my scooter a little contemptuously.

247

The instructor was a big man with a big white beard and a powerful bike.

'Ten inch wheels,' he said to me, indicating my scooter, 'that'll make getting round some of the courses a bit tricky. A lot like you don't bother, with the test.'

'Because it's tricky?'

'No, because you can ride up to a 125 on provisional, and that's all many of them want to do.'

'Oh. Do you think I'll pass?'

'I'm a good teacher,' he said, 'If you do what I say, you'll pass.'

'Have you been doing this long?' I asked in my new spirit of showing an interest in other people.

'Six or seven years,' he told me. 'I used to be in the police.'

Some of the others looked a bit apprehensive at this revelation. It seemed my new approach was already paying off.

We spent the morning weaving in and out of bollards, trying to control our machines without putting our feet down. It wasn't too hard. The figure of eight was the worst. It felt as if there should be judges holding up score cards when we'd finished. I'd have given me a 4.5. At lunchtime we sat around eating whatever we'd brought with us. I had my normal college sandwich, apple and biscuit. One lad, who introduced himself as Nigel, hadn't brought anything so I gave him half of my sandwich.

'So why are you taking your test?' I asked him.

'I want to get a big machine,' he said '500cc or so and take it round the world.'

'Wow,' I said.

'Yeah,' he said, 'you gotta think big.'

'And small,' I said. 'Don't forget to take lunch with you when you go, will you?'

He grinned. 'I'll take you with me, shall I? Then you can look after that side of things.'

He was the first to be tested round the course and although he wobbled quite a bit, he didn't put a foot down and he passed.

I was up next. I was really nervous suddenly and couldn't even get the engine started.

'Take a deep breath,' suggested the instructor.

I did and managed to get through the test successfully.

'Well done,' said Nigel.

After everyone else sailed through the test, we went out on the road. We all had yellow visibility jackets with 'Learner' written on the back so the other road users would know to give us an extremely wide berth. The instructor showed us likely places where we would be tested for emergency stop and the other elements of the part two test and explained what we would have to do.

When we got back he informed us that he thought we were all ready to take the test, although that wasn't a guarantee that we would pass.

'You need to not panic,' he told me. 'You'll have to forget that the examiner will be watching. Do that and you should be okay.'

I rode round to June's house when we were finished. Predictably she wasn't there so I went round to Ben's instead. His mum said he was asleep so I went home instead.

'I got my part one,' I told Mum.

'Ooh, well done,' she said. 'I've got an interview.'

'Already? That was quick.'

'Yes, well, they're not really recruiting so I just dropped my CV in and the manager had a look at it there and then and invited me to come back in next week.'

'Wow, Mum, well done.'

'Thanks. It doesn't mean I've got the job though. Now I have to think about something to wear. I need to look business-like which is going to be a bit of a stretch.'

'Oh, we'll find you something, Mum.'

The next week was my week at Crendell's. As I was standing in for Bob, my job was to keep the kitchen clean and wash the pans and plates and cutlery as they came back into the kitchen. It was an easy job, one that didn't involve too much stress as long as I kept up with the work and gave me lots of thinking time. As I wasn't working the counter I didn't see Dave although he would have known I was there because my scooter was parked out the front. I did want to see him, but only really to ask whether he had heard from Lance. I wondered whether they were missing him in the warehouse.

It was Wednesday before I saw Dave. I was attempting to throw some bags of rubbish into the big bins round the back of the kitchen.

'Can I help you with those?' he asked. 'I saw you struggling from my office.'

'I'm not struggling,' I said.

'No, doesn't look like it.' He took one of the bags from me and threw it easily into the bin.

'Are you alright?' he asked.

'Yes,' I said. 'How about you? Things going okay with Sam?' Now I had Dave in front of me, I was nervous of bringing up the subject of Lance.

'Yes, good, thanks. A bit all-consuming. Not much time for my mates.'

'No, well that's girls for you,' I said. 'Have you .. ?'

'Heard from Salty?' he finished for me.

'Yes.'

'No.'

'You haven't?'

'No. I've seen Perry, who's back from Dunbar. He said they had a good rally, got up there okay and all that, a few mechanical problems but nothing too serious. Then he and Salty parted ways half way back sometime on the Sunday night and that's the last anyone's heard of him. Unless you .. '

'No.'

'Oh.'

251

'So you don't know if he's going to Isle of Wight? Sam's booked him on our ferry so we really need to know. I'd phone but . .'

'No. Nothing.' In a way I was relieved that Dave hadn't heard from him. At least he wasn't keeping in touch with his mates and not with me.

'Anyway, I'd better be getting back, I've still got cleaning up to do.' I said.

'Oh, alright. Are you here all summer?' Dave asked.

'No, just this week.'

'Oh, okay. We need to sort out timings for Isle of Wight, we've got the 12.30 ferry on the Friday I think. Will you be at the Red Cow, next week?'

'Yes, probably.'

'See you there then.'

Mum had her interview at the end of the week. She was already up and attempting to do her make-up by the time I left for Crendell's.

'Don't be nervous, Mum, you're worse than me.'

'No, you're right,' she said drawing a kohl line unevenly along her upper eyelid, 'I'll be fine.'

And she was fine. When I got home she told me in great detail about what the manager had asked her and what she said in reply.

'He said I'd be an asset to the team,' she said.

'Does that mean you've got a job?' I asked.

'Not yet, I have to get the college to offer me a place on their course first.'

'More application forms then?'

'Yes. Oh, there's a letter for you here.'

It was the date for my part two test, two days after we were due back from Ibiza and two days before I was due to go to Isle of Wight. At least I could afford it, with the money from Crendell's.

Since I hadn't seen June, I phoned her up and asked her if she would meet me at the Red Cow on the following Wednesday.

'I'll come if Ben's mum say she can go too.'

'Is that likely?' I asked.

'I don't know, I'll let you know. Heard from Lance?'

'No. I thought you told me not to get hung up on whether I hear from him or not.'

'Well, yes, but I still want to know if you have.'

'Well I haven't.' It had now been more than two weeks since I had last seen him and I wasn't thinking of him as much as I had been. I wondered if I could get off with someone else if the opportunity arose. That would lay his ghost a bit, I thought. I wondered what Lance would say if I turned up at the ferry apparently with another scooterist. Still I had no guarantee that he wouldn't bring a girl down from Manchester with him. I decided to have a look around in the Red Cow Wednesday evening just to see if there was anyone likely.

June and Ben did come to the Red Cow. Ben's dad didn't want him having to deal with

253

public transport so he gave them a lift in and arranged to pick them up after.

'I'm only allowed coke,' Ben said, 'and only moderate dancing.' He seemed relieved to be out but I thought it would be a strange person who wouldn't be after nearly two months cooped up in hospital and at home.

'You know I missed my exams?' he said. It had occurred to me although we hadn't talked about it. 'The school's arranged for me to do them in November.'

'Six month's extra revision time then.'

'Yeah, I ought to do well, didn't I?'

He was treated a bit like a returning hero when he went into the pub. Even those people who would normally have ignored him for being too young came over to check he was okay. He was part of scooter rally history now – the lad who ended up in a coma after an accident at Yarmouth, but came out alive. He got several offers of a lift down to the Isle of Wight. He said he would have to see if he was allowed. I saw June trying to score herself a lift too. I had decided to keep quiet about the date for my part two. Like Tom, I didn't want to be in the position of having to admit I failed. I also thought that June might invite herself to the rally as a passenger and I wasn't sure I was ready to ride two-up or even if the scooter would be capable of it.

I went to speak to Sam about the plans for the trip down.

'We're meeting here at 8am. I know, I know,' she said when she saw me pulling a face, 'but we have to be in Portsmouth for twelve or we'll miss the ferry.'

'Any word from Lance?'

'None yet, although I'm holding his ticket for him. Let me know if you hear from him, won't you?'

I was beginning to think that this was less and less likely.

'Do you think I should be staying faithful to him?' I asked her.

'Why, do you have a replacement in mind?'

'Not as such.' I had had a look but it seemed a bit weird just trying to pick one out of a crowd. I still didn't know any of the other SeaDogs to any extent. My brief meeting with Perry hadn't marked him out as a possible partner and Bertie seemed a bit old. The others only came to the Red Cow irregularly and so I hadn't been able to figure any of them out. There were plenty of other lads about but I felt part of the Sessex Girl/SeaDog group now and decided that it would be weird going outside of it. I thought that it might lead to difficulties deciding who to go the rallies with.

'Oh well, I shouldn't worry about it then.' Dave came over as Sam said this.

'What shouldn't Annie worry about?' he asked.

'Oh, she was wondering whether she should be staying faithful to Salty. But since she hasn't got anyone to be unfaithful with, I was telling her that she didn't even need to be asking the question.'

'If you think there's anything between you two, you should definitely not be looking for anyone else.' Dave said. He looked faintly appalled at the thought. He shrugged. 'It's up to you, of course, but I would find out exactly where you stand first.'

'How am I going to do that, though?'

'Wait till Isle of Wight? He won't miss that if he can help it.'

'Don't be in such a hurry, Annie,' Sam said. Sometimes things don't make sense until much later.'

That didn't make sense, but I did think that maybe one day I might understand it.

'I'll see you on the Friday then,' I said. 'We're off to Ibiza next week.'

'Have a good time,' said Sam.

'Say no to all those Spanish barmen,' said Dave.

Chapter Twenty Two

When I got up on Saturday there was a letter waiting for me. It had a handwritten envelope and a Manchester postmark. At last, I thought, a message from Lance.

I took it upstairs and pulled out a single lined sheet of paper. It didn't say much.

'Annie,' he had written, 'See you on the Isle of Wight Ferry. Wait for me. Lance.' He had added a kiss at the end.

I read the note several times. There was no address or phone number so I couldn't contact him. I wondered what the 'wait for me' meant. Wait for him at the ferry? Or stay faithful to him? Sam had been right, since I had no one else to replace Lance, then it wasn't really an issue. But suppose I did meet someone in Ibiza. I had heard all about holiday romances from school friends who'd got off with a boy at their hotel or had met an Italian or whatever on the beach. I had made sure that I had got a decent bikini to wear so I wasn't totally forgetting the idea that someone might find me attractive.

We were due to fly from Stansted airport. It didn't seem a very glamorous place to leave from as most of the departure area seemed to be housed in a large shed. Still our plane was satisfying large and I got the window seat.

The take-off was scary. Dad sat next to me with his hands gripping the ends of the armrests, his knuckles standing out white against the rest of his hand. Once we had levelled out he said: 'Well, I'm never doing that again.'

'Dad,' I said, 'we've got to get home yet.'

'I'm going by coach,' he said firmly.

He calmed down a bit after that, but didn't eat much of the food they brought round. Mum was sat by the aisle, writing things in a notebook.

'I'll need to know what I'm talking about,' she said. 'I expect many of our customers will never have flown before.' She engaged a flight attendant in a long conversation.

'Don't think you're going for a job on a plane,' Dad warned her.

'Oh, don't worry,' she replied. 'I'm far too old and fat for a job like that.'

Neither Dad nor I were polite enough to tell her that she wasn't.

The heat hit me as soon as we got to the top of the steps at the plane door. The sun seemed much brighter than at home and it reflected off the whiteness of the runway, making it hard to see. It made me feel extraordinarily happy, as if suddenly anything was possible.

'When are we going to see Julia?' I asked Mum.

'This evening, I hope. Once we've settled in.'

We sat at the front of the coach that took us to our apartment complex. The rep who went with us was an impossibly cheerful and bouncy girl called Emily. Mum told her proudly that we had come to see Julia who had just started as a children's rep.

'Oh, we're in the same hotel,' she told us. 'She seems to be getting on fine so far. We're trying to find a role for her in the rep's show.'

'Acting?' I asked.

'Acting, singing, dancing, we do it all.' Emily said. It didn't sound very much like anything Julia was any good at.

'Can we come and watch it?' Mum asked.

'Of course,' she replied. 'The guests are who we do it for.'

Our apartment looked a bit basic but it was clean and we had a view across a road and a field to the beach.

'It said two minutes to the beach in the brochure,' said Dad. 'I reckon I could do it in one if I ran.'

'Go on then,' I goaded.

'We'll time you from here,' said Mum.

We had all changed from our English summer clothes. Mum had a flowery dress on and Dad and I had both opted for shorts, although neither of us wore them well.

It felt good to be so free of clothing. I thought back to the layers I wore on the scooter and the trip up to Yarmouth in the rain. I felt heavy and worn down just thinking about my parka hung up in my wardrobe. There were nudist beaches on the island Emily had said on the coach. I wondered if I would have the nerve to take all my clothes off in public and what it would feel like if I did. I didn't think it was something I would try in front of Mum and Dad though and I hoped it wasn't something they would try in front of me.

Emily had pointed us in the direction of Julia's hotel when we got off the bus so we had no problems finding it. We arrived just as Julia and her fellow reps were delivering the children back to their parents. Julia was talking to one mum about how her son had behaved as if she had been doing the job for years. She saw us and waved.

'Emily said you were here,' she said when she managed to get over to us.

'How are you getting on, love?' Mum asked. 'Did you make the right decision?'

'Yes Mum, I think I did,' Julia replied happily. 'You know I think I really like kids.'

She showed us round the hotel and we ate in the restaurant there.

'It's one of the company's flagship hotels,' Julia said, 'so everyone here apart from the hotel staff is British and even most of them speak can good English.'

'So you won't have to learn the language then?' Dad asked.

'Most reps know a few words. 'Cerveza' I've learned, that's beer. And por favor and gracias, but no one seems to expect you to know more than that.'

'What about the Spanish?' I asked. 'Wouldn't it be polite to know more so you can speak to them?'

Julia shrugged. 'If you get a Spanish boyfriend maybe. But most of my time is spent with the kids and with the other reps so I don't really have the opportunity anyway.' I thought that it was a shame to pass up on the chance to learn the language from those who spoke it, but I didn't say so.

We arranged to meet the next evening after Julia had finished work. 'We'll go up to the old town, she said. You won't believe the place, it's wild.'

Mum, Dad and I walked back to our apartment. I listened to passers-by to see if I could work out where they came from. Most of them were British, but I heard a few German voices. Nothing that sounded Spanish though. I wondered if they avoided these resorts outside of work. I wouldn't have blamed them. There were gangs of beery lads and families with kids who seemed to have been out in the sun too long. I looked at my own skin. Much as I wanted a tan to return home with, I was going to have to be careful, already I was looking a bit pink.

The next day I slathered on the sun cream and we went to explore our local area. It was mostly hotels and apartments, cafes and bars and shops selling handbags and perfume. The beach however was wide and pale yellow in colour and stretched out for miles in either direction. The sea was clear and pale blue. We wandered down to where the beach met some cliffs and Dad bought a snorkel set and we took it in turns to paddle about looking for exotic fish in the shallows.

Mum had a book and settled herself under a shade to read it.

'Don't think you have to stay with us, Annie,' she said. 'You might want to go off and explore on your own.'

'I might in a bit,' I replied.

For the moment, I was quite happy to sit and admire the view. We were on a beach, like Lance and I were on a beach at Clacton, but the similarities ended with the location. Even though many of the people on the beach were British, this was nothing like the English seaside. I couldn't even see children building sandcastles. Maybe it wasn't the right sort of sand. Or maybe it was the heat. It seemed to take away the desire to do anything. I lay down on my towel and dozed off.

I awoke much later, dry mouthed and headachy.

'Too much sun and not enough to drink,' said Dad as we made our way into the shade of a bar.

That evening we met up with Julia and she took us by bus into Ibiza Town.

'We're a bit early,' she said as we walked through narrow streets with bars and restaurants on either side that seemed to be just opening up for the evening. We chose a restaurant with red checked tablecloths and sat down.

'Hola,' Mum said to the waiter. 'See, I know a bit of Spanish,' she whispered to us.

The menu was written in Spanish with English and German translations underneath. I went for pasta with clams which was a mistake because they were still in their shells and I had to extract each one individually. We had a bottle of wine between us and Mum, Julia and I soon got giggly.

In the time we had sat in the restaurant, the area had filled up and there was a constant stream of people walking past our table.

'You said this place was wild,' said Mum who seemed to be a bit disappointed that most of the passers-by were tourists like us.

'You haven't seen behind you, though,' I said. I pointed over to a restaurant on the other side of the street where an older man in heavy make-up was sitting surrounded by a group of beautiful younger boys all feeding each other from their own plates.

'Is that a man or a woman?' Dad asked.

'It's a man, Dad,' said Julia. There's lots of them like that here. They're all very flamboyant.' Dad shuddered.

'I suppose they have to come to places like this,' said Mum. 'We're not very tolerant in our country are we?'

Once we had eaten, Julia took us to the top of the old town where there was a small square in front of a cathedral. I sat down on a wall. From there you could see the whole of the town and the harbour laid out below. It looked ancient in a way that the places I visited regularly did not. Houses were crammed next to each other. It looked as though the builders had started with one house at one end and added another and another each time a new family had come along. Some of the houses were expansive with big windows and substantial doorways but most of them were tiny. We could hear the sounds of children's games so it seemed likely that families lived there.

I wondered what their lives were like. I tried to imagine myself living there and could not. I thought I would always be out of step with how the other inhabitants thought and felt. This made me feel depressed, as if I had no choice in who or what I could be. Even Julia, I thought, wasn't going to change so much that she wouldn't be first and foremost a girl from England. Those men in the restaurant were still who they always were underneath all the make-up and gaudy clothing. They were just trying harder than the rest of us to be someone else.

Suddenly I felt trapped in my body, in my femaleness and my Englishness. I had never thought much about being English before, but here it didn't seem such a great thing to be. I wanted to lose my identity and become nation-less and gender-less if such a thing were possible.

I wondered if there was a way of forgetting all your past in order to start again somewhere new without any ideas brought in from a previous life. But you couldn't wipe your mind clean, I thought. Even Ben in his coma had come out the other side the same old Ben, a bit more fragile perhaps, but otherwise unchanged.

Dad came and sat down beside me.

'It's beautiful here, isn't it?' he said. 'Makes me wonder why we took so long to come out this way.'

'Because you have to fly to get here?' I suggested.

'Ah yes,' he said, 'there is that. I'm not looking forward to doing that again.'

'Maybe it'll be easier the second time.'

'Yes,' said Dad. 'Perhaps.'

Poor old Dad, I thought. In my mind he was a sort of solid presence. Anything I couldn't handle I could pass on to him. But in some ways he was just as weak as the rest of us, with his choices restricted by the things that scared him. It didn't make me love him any less though. He was my Dad after all and some things, I thought, are non-negotiable.

The next day Julia had a day off and had arranged for us to go on a boat trip.

'It goes to Formentera,' she said. 'I haven't been on it yet, so I'm really excited.'

Kez, one of the reps from Julia's hotel came along as well. She seemed to have attracted a hoard of men who all seemed to have come on holiday together.

'They're a rugby team,' she told me. 'They come away somewhere every year. I met them two years ago and kept in touch with a couple of them and this year they found out where I was based and came back to see me.'

'Are they all single?' I asked.

'No, most of them are married or have got partners, but this is their boys' week away. Some of them aren't allowed to come, their wives don't let them, but that doesn't sit well with the lads I don't think.'

They seemed very polite and took Julia and I under their wing immediately. They kept us supplied with drinks on the boat and told us jokes that made us blush. When we got to Formentera they led us up the beach to a quiet spot where they set up camp and organised a series of games.

Kez, Julia and I watched the rugby game but got roped in on the cricket. I was apprehensive about joining in as I didn't want to show myself up but they gave me another go when I was bowled out first ball and after that I managed a couple of hits and a couple of runs. Mum and Dad came along the beach to see how we were doing and got roped in as well.

I was having so much fun I didn't want the afternoon to end, but, too soon the boat's horns sounded and we had to run back along the beach so they didn't go without us. I was getting left behind so one of the lads stopped and gave me a piggy-back back to the boat.

The boatmen had been cooking up huge pans of paella and we all tucked in as we sailed back to Ibiza Town.

'So,' said Col, one of the older members of the team, 'what are we doing this evening?'

'We?' asked Julia.

'Well you're all invited to whatever we decide of course,' he said.

'Pacha?' Julia suggested hopefully.

'We're not nightclub kind of people really,' Col said. 'Well most of us aren't. We prefer a quality restaurant and a bar with good beers.'

'I know a nice Spanish restaurant in Figueretas,' said Kez.

'With room for 16 or so at one table?'

'Probably.'

Mum and Dad decided to take the opportunity to have a meal on their own and so I went to meet Julia, Kez and the lads at their hotel and we all walked up the road into Figueretas together. On the way I got talking to Brian, another of the older team members. He told me he was a school teacher: 'Chemistry to teenagers.'

'Sounds like fun.'

'It can be, at times. What about you?'

So I told him about going to college, I told him about my scooter and I even told him about Lance.

'He's probably just a bit confused,' Brian said, 'most lads are at that age. He hasn't got a purpose yet. And neither have you, by the sounds of it'

'So I'm a bit confused too?'

'Well, directionless might be a better description,' he told me. 'I see it all the time in my school. There are a few kids who know what they want to do. They've got a talent or a passion for something. But there are many, many more who haven't found what it is they're good at.'

'Well I am doing catering.'

'Ah, but do you love it? Do you wake up in the morning wondering what you're going to do with the cabbage when you get in the kitchen?'

'Not really. I like making bread though and I love making puddings.'

'Well, there you go. Maybe you should be studying patisserie instead of general catering.'

'I didn't know you could do that.'

'I don't know that you can, but patissiers have to learn somewhere don't they? You should take yourself off to France and get an apprenticeship in a pastry shop there, learn from a pro.'

'Can you do that?'

'Why not?

'I'd probably need to learn French first.'

'Yes. Well at least the words that are relevant to making pastry.'

'And what about Lance, what should he be doing?'

'He should be fixing up scooters probably. Oh and he should come back and claim you while he still has the chance.'

'Yeah,' I said, 'and he'd better hurry up or I'll be off making éclairs in Paris.'

Chapter Twenty Three

The next day Dad hired a car and we drove to some of the other resorts. Mum had her notebook out and was taking notes the whole time.

'You'll be sending everyone to Ibiza,' Dad said to her.

'Well, why not?' she replied, 'and now I'll be able to tell them which resort is best for them.'

I was pleased she was so into this potential new job. I hoped she got the college place. I told her what Brian had said about finding something I was really interested in.

'Well isn't that what college is for?' she asked. 'You try new things and see what you really enjoy. Then you have to find out if you can do it for a living. You shouldn't be in too much of a hurry to decide, you know. How you think at sixteen is very different to how you think at thirty and you might end up stuck doing something you hate.'

'But that leaves me directionless.'

'Or it leaves you open to opportunities. There's more than one way of looking at things you know,' she said.

Later, we returned to the beach near our apartment. I had bought a lilo and I cast it out on to the sea and lay on it, directing myself lazily with a bit of sculling. I imagined myself slowly floating out to sea on it, just gently disappearing, no one noticing that I had gone. I was so lost in my thoughts that I didn't realise that I had drifted down the coast some way. I heaved myself off the lilo and swam with it back to the beach, walking back up until I found Mum and Dad.

'There you are,' said Dad. 'We'd lost you, I was just about to organise the search party.'

'You did say I could go off exploring on my own.'

'Yes, not by sea though,' said Mum, 'you must have some sense.'

The rugby lads were due to return home on Saturday so they organised a big meal for everyone they'd met over the week. There were so many of us we ended up taking over most of the garden of a big local restaurant.

'How did you meet so many people?' I asked Col.

'Well there's a lot of us to begin with. And we just like collecting people. We like to share the joy that comes with being a member of our team.'

'It sounds like a good way of thinking.'

'It is.'

I was sad to see them go. I nearly went and waved them off on their coach. Julia said that she had and it had taken so long for them to get on board the rep was fretting about them missing the plane.

The island seemed a little emptier once I knew they had gone. We only had two days left ourselves though and suddenly a week didn't seem long enough. On Sunday I decided that I would go exploring myself and took the bus into Ibiza Town again.

All of the shops were shut up and only a few of the cafes were open. It seemed very lonely but also more real as if the shops were just like the make-up we saw on the man in the restaurant. I climbed up to the cathedral again. Its bell was tolling slowly and I watched as mostly elderly ladies dressed in black made their way inside. This was reality for them, I thought. I wondered what they had seen in their lives. Every one of them, I thought, would have some interesting story to tell.

Here I did not feel conspicuous. I felt invisible and it felt good. As a tourist I was not important to these people. They would be grateful for my custom but not interested in my life which meant that it didn't matter who I was.

I wandered back down through the narrow streets. Here and there the locals were stood in doorways, having conversations. I listened in to them as I went past, enjoying the fact that they made no sense to me. Their speech was fast and some used gestures to emphasise what they were saying, using their whole body to tell the story.

Back on the harbour I sat and watched the boats coming and going. There were some flashy looking yachts moored on the other side. We had seen some when we'd been on the boat trip. Each one seemed to have a woman in a bikini laid out on the front of it, like a car ornament. I wondered if that was their job, perhaps they got paid to make the owner look even more successful than ownership of a very expensive boat might already suggest. Of course, I thought, the women could be the boat owners but somehow it didn't seem very likely.

I thought perhaps I could get a job on one of these boats, cooking or cleaning or something. If it was something I really wanted to do, I thought, I should go over there and ask. That's what Brian would tell me to do, I was sure.

Looking at the boats made me think about Nigel, the lad I'd met on the motorcycle training course. I wondered if he would actually take off and travel the world on a bike. So many people, I thought, just talked about their dreams but, when it came to it, found excuses not to see them through. Perhaps it was best not get fixed on one thing, then it wouldn't look as though you'd failed when the thing you said you really wanted didn't happen.

I went in a shop to buy an ice cream. I decided to try out some of the little Spanish I had learnt.

'Un helado, por favor,' I said

'Large or small?' asked the shop assistant.

'How did you know I was English?' I asked him.

'Oh, I can tell,' he replied.

On our last night, we had a last meal together as a family and then Julia and I hit the bars.

'Will you miss us when we're gone?' I asked.

'Well of course I will,' she said. 'But I'm quite glad you're going too. I've just met all these new people and I want to spend my free time with them, really. I want to do nineteen year old stuff. I want to stay out until 3 am and then go straight to do an airport transfer. Oh, and I don't want people questioning whether I'm doing the right thing.'

'No one's done that, have they?' I asked.

'Not in so many words, but sometimes you can just sense disapproval, or at least concern. When I come home in October, I want to be able to tell you about some of the highlights of my summer and keep everything else to myself.'

'Are you thinking of cheating on Barry?' I asked. 'Is that what it's all about?'

'Oh I won't cheat on Barry, because we won't be together. Even a month away from home has taught me that. I'm not nearly ready for all that responsibility.'

'Does he know that yet?'

'No, but I expect he's thinking the same thing himself. We were trying too hard to be adults, that's all.'

'He's not coming out to see you then?'

'No, I hope not. That would be embarrassing.'

'I'll tell him that if I see him, shall I?'

'If you like.'

Julia had asked her supervisor to be allowed to be the rep on our coach back to the airport. She had to give a speech on the microphone telling us all the checking in procedure. She sounded very professional and when someone ahead of us had a problem with his ticket, I thought that she handled it very well. I figured she would make a success of this job, despite all her talk of not being ready to be an adult.

Mum got a bit emotional when we had to say goodbye.

'Mum, I'm only two and a half hours away by plane. If you get that job, you'll get concessions and you can come out every weekend if you want to.'

I knew Julia would hate this if Mum actually decided to do it, but I thought it was a nice thing to say. We hugged and said goodbye at the departure gate but Julia did not stand and watch us go as we had done with her. She was immediately back off down the steps to get ready for the new arrivals.

Stansted was grey and gloomy when we arrived back.

'I thought it was supposed to be August,' grumbled Dad. He had to be at work the next day so I couldn't blame his mood.

Mum was much happier because she had her college interview at the end of the week. I had my part two test in two days and the Isle of Wight rally at the end of the week.

There was a bit of post on the doormat at home, but nothing from Lance. I wasn't really expecting anything. He seemed very distant to me. Distant and dull-coloured after the light and brightness of Ibiza. I wondered if I never saw him again if I would be okay with that. I felt I needed to see him to see if I got that strange pull in my stomach at the sight of him.

The following day I pulled my scooter out from the garage where we stored it while we went away. It too looked a little strange after a week away. It looked like nothing you would ever think of inventing if it didn't already exist.

Still I needed to pass my test so I took it out on a test run, making sure that everything worked and that I could still remember how to ride it. I took it down the Causeway, a long straight road out to the marshes where lads would have races in or on whatever vehicle they had managed to get hold of. There was hardly anyone else around and I gunned the scooter up and down for a bit.

I wished I knew circus skills and could stand up and balance, no hands, while still keeping the scooter running straight. I wished I had some extraordinary skill like that, that I could show to others and have them marvel at my talent. But I didn't. There wasn't anything that I could think of that marked me out as special or even interesting. I could understand why boys would invent superhero powers, something to make them stand out from the crowd and be the one who everyone admired.

I didn't sleep very well that night. This was like an exam and exams always made me nervous. I had to be at the test centre by twelve and was there not much after eleven. I sat on my scooter in the car park and watched people taking their car tests come and go. I saw two people pass while I sat there and the look of happiness and relief on their faces when they got out of their cars gave me the impetus to try and do my best myself.

I went inside to tell them I had arrived and waited for the examiner. He was an older man, not very chatty so we just got on with the test. I seemed to answer his questions correctly and he sent me off on a route while he stood on a corner and watched me turning corners while making marks on a clipboard. We did the emergency stop down a side street. He stepped out in front of me and I managed both not to run him over or to go flying over the handlebars.

After about half an hour's worth of being observed I rode back to the test centre to await his verdict.

'Well, Miss Morrish, I am pleased to tell you that you have passed.'

I smiled, relieved that I had achieved the grade. When he had signed and handed over the forms and gone back inside I made a little ceremony of removing my L plates. They didn't tear up because they were made of plastic so I stuffed them in my glove box instead. The scooter looked much better without them, more grown up, I thought.

I decided to ride into town to see if June was at Debenhams. I couldn't see her but decided to stop and have a cup of tea anyway. As I was paying she came out of the kitchen with a tray of cakes.

'Hey, nice tan,' she said

'Thanks,' I said doing a little twirl, 'does it suit me?'

'Yes. It makes you irresistible. Have a nice time, did you?'

'Fantastic, thanks. And I've got some other news, I just passed my motorbike test.' I hadn't been planning to tell her. I had wanted to see if she noticed the absence of L plates, but I needed to tell somebody.

'Wow,' she said, 'really? Congratulations. Can you give me a lift home?'

'Got a helmet?' I asked.

'Not on me.'

'No, then. Soz and all.' I was relieved, I wasn't quite ready for a passenger and I didn't want to hang around town all afternoon waiting for her to finish. I went and sat at a table and she followed me and sat down too.

'Are you allowed?' I asked.

'Yeah, the manager's gone to Benidorm for a fortnight so we're all taking it easy. I could see what she meant, there were dirty cups and plates piled on most of the tables.

'So are you ready for Isle of Wight?' she asked me.

'I think so, as I'll ever be. Did you manage to get a lift?'

'Yes. Perry's taking me. He's charging me a pretty hefty price for petrol I thought but I'm loaded after all this work so I don't care.'

'What about Ben?'

'He's going with Dave. His Dad finally gave in and said he could go. He realised that he couldn't wrap him in cotton wool forever.'

'I'd have thought that Dave was a pretty reliable person to go with,' I said. 'That is if he has forgiven Ben for shagging Sam at Morecambe.'

'Oh, yes,' said June, 'I'd forgotten about that.'

'I bet Dave hasn't.'

'Hey, you could take someone now,' June said. 'Undercut Perry and you could take me or find some little Mod who's desperate to go and you could clean up on what you charge them for petrol.'

'I'm not sure my scooter would make it all the way down there two-up I said. We'd probably only manage 30 miles an hour.'

'Yeah, I suppose.' June answered. 'Are you going to trade up now? Get yourself something with a bit more poke?'

'I've got no plans,' I said. 'Maybe if something comes up. I'm quite attached to old Luigi really.'

'So did you meet anyone in Ibiza?' June asked.

'I met a whole rugby team. But I didn't get off with any of them, if that's what you mean.'

'Oh, why not?'

'Because I decided to wait and see what happens with Lance and me. If anything.'

'And what if it's nothing?'

'Then I move on. If you don't have a boyfriend you've got a lot more freedom. I could go to Paris and train to be a patissier if I wanted. For instance.'

'Ah, but would you?'

'I could, as I am only limited by the paucity of my dreams,' I said dramatically.

'What?'

'Yeah, I don't know what it means either. Sounds good though, I think, don't you?'

'Yeah,' said June, 'Whatever. Look I'd better go and do some work. I'll see you the day after tomorrow then, 8am at the Red Cow.'

'Are you looking forward to it?' I asked.

'You betcha,' she said.

Chapter Twenty Four

I packed all my stuff for Isle of Wight on Thursday evening so I could just get up and go on the Friday morning. Mum was up before me and had made sandwiches which she wrapped in foil and forced on me.

'I don't have any space for sandwiches,' I told her.

'Put them in your pocket or something,' she said. 'I'm concerned you don't eat right on these trips.'

'Well maybe I could fit them inside my helmet, like Paddington.' I said.

'If you want marmalade in your hair, I suppose you could. Look just humour me and squeeze them in somewhere. You might be glad of them.'

'Okay Mum. I've got to go. I'll be back on Monday evening sometime I expect.'

'Oh, right. Aren't you going to wish me luck?'

'Oh yes, sorry Mum. You'll be fine. Tell them all about Ibiza.' I had forgotten it was her college interview. I was too wrapped up in myself again.

It was a sunny day, but I felt a bit of a chilly breeze round my neck as I set off. It was at least three-layer weather I thought. I had five layers on my top half because it gave me more choice of clothes than I could carry on the back of my scooter. There were already a few yellow leaves on the trees, a sign that autumn was on the way. I wanted to cling on to summer as long as I could, I wasn't ready for the shorter days yet.

As I headed into town I realised that I was hunched over the handle bars. I tried to tense and relax each part of my body in turn, not an easy thing to do when you're riding at 50 miles an hour on two wheels. I knew that I was tense because of Lance. I had read his letter over and over again the night before and I was carrying it in the inside pocket of my jacket like some sort of lucky charm. I hadn't needed to read it of course, I knew what it said. I was just hoping that somehow I would be able to interpret the meaning of the sentence 'Wait for me'.

As I rode up to the Red Cow, I could see a number of scooters in the car park already. I parked up alongside Karen who was struggling with her luggage.

'I think I've brought too much,' she said as I helped her tie it on safely.

'Someone should have a trailer or something,' I said.

All the girls were there along with Dave and a couple of the other SeaDogs. Sam was taking Andrea whose scooter was not up to the journey.

Dave came over. 'Hello,' he said. 'Have you lost the L plates?'

'Permanently,' I replied, 'I passed my test.'

'Congratulations,' he said, giving me a hug. 'Are you trading up?'

'Not immediately.'

'You should, I bet you could sell yours on easily enough.'

Sam came along with photocopies of a hand-drawn map.

'Did you know Annie's passed her test?' Dave said to her.

'No? You kept that quiet,' she said. 'Well done. Anyway here's the map of the route in case you get lost. You shouldn't though, I've got Dave and Perry riding up front and Bertie at the rear in case anyone falls behind.'

'You're very organised.' I said.

'Yes, isn't she?' said Dave. 'I don't know how we managed to get to a rally before we teamed up with you girls.'

Sam elbowed him in the ribs 'We should all be here now,' she said as another couple of scooters showed up.

'What about Ben and June?' I asked.

'They're just coming up the road.'

I looked up and saw them walking together. As they got closer I could see they were holding hands.

I waited until they had got into the car park and then cornered June.

'What's that all about?' I asked her.

'What's all what all about?' she asked innocently.

'You know. The hand-holding.'

'Ah, you spotted that, did you? Well we've spent so much time together over the summer and we've discovered that we really like each other's company. Anyway, last night my Mum and Dad were out and we sealed the deal.'

'No!' I hadn't anticipated that.

'Yeah, and,' she moved in to whisper in my ear, 'he's very good. Much better than Tom. I don't know why Sam didn't hold on to him.'

'Oh. Well, I'm really pleased for you.' I said and I found out when I said it that I was.

Ben came over. 'You heard?' he asked, grinning.

'Yes,' I said, 'and I think you make a lovely couple.' He was holding a very smart looking helmet. He saw me looking at it and tapped it with his knuckles.'

'Latest technology,' he told me. 'My dad bought it for me. He's not very keen on me coming so he's doing his best to makes sure I come back safely.'

'You'll be okay,' I said.

'I will with this on,' he replied.

'Ten minutes,' Sam shouted and we all began to make our preparations to leave.

'I'm going to the loo, before anyone reminds me to go,' I said to June. She went over to Perry to stow her stuff on his scooter.

One by one we all started up our scooters and got ready to go. Dave with Ben on the back pulled away first, followed by Perry with June. She had her hands on the back rest and her feet stretched out in front. She looked pretty comfortable and gave me a wave as they left the car park.

I kicked my scooter off the stand and pulled away behind Sarah and Suzy. There were seven

283

scooters in front of me and three behind. The sight of all our scooters all piled up with riders and tents passing through the town made many people look. People on their way to work, I thought. It felt good to be part of it, in the middle of the pack.

We headed west then south, aiming for the Dartford Tunnel. After a while we stretched out a bit, making a long chain of a quarter of a mile or so. In the tunnel there was much whooping and shouting. I joined in, making as much noise as I could. Out the other side, we paid the toll and rode out into the sunlight. For a time we merged with another smaller group of scooters and there was a bit of high-spirited jockeying for place. We lost them though when we pulled over at a petrol station.

'Breakfast stop,' said Sam and we all wandered into the shop for drinks and food. I sat down on a patch of grass and pulled my sandwiches out to eat. Dave and Sam came and sat next to me. June and Ben were snogging by the car wash.

'Have you heard from Lance?' Dave asked me.

'I had a letter, before I went away.'

'Did it say much?'

'He said he'd see us on the ferry. And that was about it really. How about you?'

'We didn't hear from him at all. So in the end Sam phoned to ask if he wanted the ferry ticket and he was a bit, well, odd.'

'How do you mean?'

'He didn't seem to want to talk,' said Sam. 'He was very quiet, I could hardly get two words out of him, but at the same time, I didn't think he wanted me to hang up.'

'Oh. When was this?'

'Beginning of last week.'

'Do you think he's okay?' I asked.

'We don't know,' said Dave, 'that's why we hoped you'd had more luck.'

'No. I wondered whether to tell them about the 'Wait for me' that he'd written but it didn't seem to answer anything so I decided to keep it to myself.

'Oh, well. We should be seeing him in a couple of hours, shouldn't we?' I said. 'Perhaps everything will be clear then.'

'Yes, but if he's not at the ferry terminal, I'm not waiting for him,' said Sam.

I am, I thought to myself.

We got going again, scooting through Surrey and on into Hampshire. It was a long ride, but enjoyable, certainly the best I had been on. I began thinking about getting a new scooter. Everyone seemed to think it was the next move after passing my test. I wondered what to go for. Not a new one this time, that was certain. Maybe something classic from the sixties or even a Lambretta like Mum used to have. Really though, apart from the novelty of having something new, I didn't want to change my scooter. I felt at one with it, like it, no he, was my friend. I would be upset if I sold him on and the next owner ill-treated him. I gave him a little pat on the top of the headlight casing,

'Thanks Luigi,' I said. 'You're more than just metal.'

Chapter Twenty Five

We got to the outskirts of Portsmouth without incident and followed the signs for the port. Dave was in charge of leading us. He seemed to get a bit lost and we ended up riding down the front at Southsea past acres of green grass and kids with candy floss on sticks. He stopped to check the map and we all pulled up and grouped around him.

'We can't be that far,' said Sarah, 'I can see a boat leaving up ahead.' We all looked where she was pointing to see a ferry steaming out into the river.

'I hope that's not ours,' said Suzy.

'No, we've got an hour yet,' replied Sam.

Up ahead, I could see something else, someone crouched down in front of a green scooter that was resting on its side on an area of grass.

'It looks like there's someone broken down up there,' I said to Dave.

He looked over. 'That's not Lance is it?' he asked.

We were too far away to be sure but it did look like his scooter.

'I'll go and see,' said Sam and she started her scooter up and rode off towards him as we all watched. She pulled up and leaned over to speak to the person who looked up briefly and then went back to fiddling with his engine. Sam looked over at us and waved us over. We all rode up and parked up in a neat row as if this was the rally and we were showing off our machines.

I hung back as the others surrounded Lance but I saw him look for me and smiled at him as we locked eyes. He didn't smile back.

'It's fucking dead,' I heard him say as he stood up and gave the scooter a kick. 'I've pushed it three miles just to get it here.'

The lads all got down in front of the scooter and began looking it over. June came over to me, stretching her legs out one at a time.

'I've seized up,' she complained.

'Looks like Lance's scooter has too,' I said.

'Yeah, shouldn't you be in there, mopping his brow and smoothing things over?'

'I think I'll stay out of it for now.'

'Doesn't look like he's going anywhere though, does it?' June asked.

There was a food stall nearby so we walked over and bought coffees. I got an extra one for Lance, which I carried over and placed by his side.

'Coffee there for you,' I said.

'Thanks,' He looked up and me and touched me briefly on the arm with an oil-stained hand.

'S'alright.' I moved away again.

After another ten minutes fiddling about, Sam started to get antsy. Looking at her watch she said: 'We're going to have to go in a minute if we're going to make this ferry.'

The boys all looked up at her. Obviously no one wanted to miss the ferry, but I didn't think they wanted to leave Lance scooter-less either.

'Well, look,' said Dave, 'we've got to be practical. Some of you at least had better go for the ferry.'

'And then what are you going to do?' Sam asked.

'Try and get on another one, I suppose.' Dave answered

'And suppose you can't? Or you can't fix Salty's scooter.'

'We won't fix it,' Salty said, 'I told you, it's dead.'

'Well someone had better give you a lift then,' said Sam. 'Who's got a spare seat?'

No one spoke. It looked as though all those with scooters able to ride two-up already had a passenger.

'Wait a minute,' said Dave, 'what about Annie?'

'What about Annie?' said Lance suspiciously.

'She's passed her test. Haven't you?' he said, looking at me.

I nodded in reply.

'Since when?' Lance asked.

'Since two days ago,' I replied.

'She won't be ready to take a passenger,' Perry said. He was right but I thought his assessment of me was a bit dismissive.

'I'll take you,' I said. Lance just looked at me.

'You happy with that, Salty?' Dave asked.

Lance sort of nodded and shrugged at the same time.

'Right.' said Dave. 'Well I don't suppose you want to leave your scooter here, or there'll be nothing left of it by the time we get back, so you'd best push it to the terminal and we'll find somewhere to leave it there. You can walk on to the ferry.'

Lance didn't say anything but just started pushing his scooter in the direction of the terminal and the rest of us started up our scooters, caught him up and then passed him.

The ferry was loading by the time we got there so we handed in our tickets and rode straight on, parking up alongside the twenty or so scooters already on board. I watched to see if Lance appeared. He did so and after speaking to one of the staff, parked his scooter around the back of one of the terminal buildings. He walked on to the ferry and was surrounded by the other SeaDogs, all wanting to ask him questions. Probably mechanical ones I thought, rather than personal.

I walked over to the side and leaned over it. I wanted to talk to him but I wanted it to be just us, not in a group. The ferry closed its doors and started its journey into the Solent. I focussed on the white water that was being thrown up along the sides of the boat, concentrating on the patterns that were being endlessly created and immediately lost.

June came over.

'You okay?' she asked.

'Yes,' I said still keeping my eyes on the water.

'Not talking to Salty?'

'Not with an audience.'

'Shall I get him to come over?' she asked.

I shook my head. 'There's plenty of time.'

Seeing that I didn't have much else to say, she gave my shoulder a brief squeeze and walked off to the front of the boat where Ben was chatting to some scooterists that we didn't know.

Left alone, I made the most of having my head free from the helmet. I shook my hair out and let the breeze catch it so it whipped around my face. I didn't see Lance approaching.

'Hello,' he said. I jumped.

'Oh, hi,' I said, not quite looking him in the face now we were so close. No one seemed to have followed him. For the moment we were all alone.

'Is it okay, you giving me a lift?' he asked.

I nodded.

'I could drive and you could be the passenger, if you thought that was better,' he said.

I shook my head. 'My scooter,' I said, 'I'll drive.'

'Okay,'

'Anyway,' I said after a moment, 'I reckon you'll be a good passenger.'

He smiled. 'You never said you were taking your test.'

'Well last time I spoke to you I wasn't,' I said, 'but that was more than a month ago. Lots has happened since then.'

'Yeah,' he replied softly, 'to me too.'

'I got your letter though,' I said. 'What did you mean, 'Wait for me'?'

'Wasn't it obvious?'

'No. It could have meant wait for you at the ferry or it could have meant . . .'

'Don't get off with anyone else?' he finished for me.

'Exactly, so which one was it?'

'Well both, but the second one mostly,' he said.

'Oh. Well I did. Wait for you, that is.'

'You did? Even in Ibiza?'

'Yeah, even though I met a whole rugby team who all wanted my body. No, I told them, I'm waiting for Salty.'

'And what did they say?'

'They said that was the right thing to do. They were quite nice about it, really.'

'Good.' He went quiet.

'So,' I asked, 'what happened to you?'

'With the scooter?'

'No. Since I last saw you.'

'Well, Dunbar was a good laugh. Lots of Scots, you know.'

'And your Dad's?'

'Not so good.'

'Oh?'

'No. It was kind of why I haven't been in touch. It all went a bit wrong.'

'With the job? Or with your Dad?'

'Both,' he said. 'I went up there thinking I had a room, but apparently it involved one of my sister's moving into the other one's room. Which she refused to do. So I ended up sleeping on the sofa. Which of course pissed everyone off. And I never did get my stuff sent up so I only had the clothes I had for Dunbar. And then it turned out that the job was only casual, so sometimes there was work and sometimes there wasn't. And I've spent the last ten days with nothing to do, annoying the hell out of Sheila, and wishing I'd never gone up there.'

'Why didn't you come home? Back to your mum's, I mean.'

'Because we kind of fell out the day before I went. She thought I wasn't treating you very well. She said I should have ridden with you back home or something rather than leave you as soon as Perry showed up.'

'Oh. Was that why you phoned?'

'Yeah, she was making me apologise. Anyway you weren't there, so I didn't get to apologise so she went off on one about how I was never going to amount to anything blah-blah-blah and she was glad I was going to my dad's because she was washing her hands of me.'

'So you didn't have anywhere to come back to?'

'Nope, or a job. I did try writing to you several times but it never came out right, since I didn't think you'd thought I'd mistreated you anyway and the point of apologising was to get mum off my back. So I just wrote that stupid note instead.'

'Oh.' That was a lot of information to get my head round. 'So what now?'

'I don't know,' Lance said. 'My mum doesn't want me, my dad and his family don't want me and I don't have a job. Oh, and as of two hours ago I don't have a scooter either.'

I thought for a moment. In front of the boat I could see the island fast approaching. Some of the scooterists were beginning to get their things together ready for the off. 'You do have me though,' I said, 'if you want me, that is.'

'Do I?'

'Yes, it's not much I know, but it's the best I can offer.'

'It'll do,' he replied. 'It's a start. Something to build on.'

'The road taken,' I said. He gave me a questioning look. 'It's from a conversation I had with my dad. He could probably get you a job on the post you know.'

'Maybe I should do what my mum says, get some qualifications, do a mechanics course or something.'

'And fix scooters for a living. It's what you have a talent for.'

'Yeah, I have thought about it. It's no good if I can't fix my own though is it?'

'I bet you could. With the right tools and all that. You can't do anything properly by the side of the road, can you?'

We began walking over to my scooter. 'Make it your measure,' I suggested, 'if you can fix it when you get home, then that shows you've got a talent for it and you should make a career out of it. Get a little shop somewhere and I'll set up a tea room in the back. We could be the first scooter repair cum coffee shop in the country.'

'Steady now, one step at a time,' he said. But he did look happier and sounded a little more normal.

We took his tent and bag over to the scooters and distributed it as best we could among the group. The ferry was getting ready to dock and many of the scooters were already ticking over ready to go.

'You'd better get on first,' I said.

'Okay, but only if you let me do this. He bent down and kissed me gently, then more forcibly as I kissed him back. His hands were still oily but it didn't matter, I took them and wrapped them around me. There was much whooping from the others around us.

'Good on you, Annie,' I heard June shout.

We broke away, embarrassed but grinning. We put our helmets on and I kick started the scooter. Lance got on leaving me room in front. I dropped the scooter off the stand and held it there, testing the balance, feeling Lance's weight behind me. The scooters in front started to pull away and I opened the throttle, letting the clutch out slowly so we moved away smoothly. I squeezed my bottom into the space between Lance's legs and he grabbed hold of my waist.

We had to do more work, my scooter and I, to accommodate Lance, but it felt good, as though we had a purpose.

We followed the stream of scooters as they led the way out of town and into the countryside. I didn't know where we were going, but for the moment I was happy just to go with the flow.

Printed in Great Britain
by Amazon.co.uk, Ltd.,
Marston Gate.